D0661106

*The Aluminum
Christmas Tree*

The Aluminum Christmas Tree

>> A Novel <<

Thomas J. Davis

Steeple
Hill®

Published by Steeple Hill Books™

If you purchased this book without a cover you should be aware that this book is stolen property. It was reported as "unsold and destroyed" to the publisher, and neither the author nor the publisher has received any payment for this "stripped book."

STEEPLE HILL BOOKS

Steeple
Hill®

Recycling programs
for this product may
not exist in your area.

ISBN-13: 978-0-373-78671-8

THE ALUMINUM CHRISTMAS TREE

Steeple Hill Books/October 2010

First published by Rutledge Hill Press

Copyright © 2005 by Thomas J. Davis

All rights reserved. Except for use in any review, the reproduction or utilization of this work in whole or in part in any form by any electronic, mechanical or other means, now known or hereafter invented, including xerography, photocopying and recording, or in any information storage or retrieval system, is forbidden without the written permission of the editorial office, Steeple Hill Books, 233 Broadway, New York, NY 10279 U.S.A.

This is a work of fiction. Names, characters, places and incidents are either the product of the author's imagination or are used fictitiously, and any resemblance to actual persons, living or dead, business establishments, events or locales is entirely coincidental.

This edition published by arrangement with Steeple Hill Books.

® and TM are trademarks of Steeple Hill Books, used under license. Trademarks indicated with ® are registered in the United States Patent and Trademark Office, the Canadian Trade Marks Office and in other countries.

www.SteepleHill.com

Printed in U.S.A.

For Terry, who helped in so many ways

*The Aluminum
Christmas Tree*

Chapter 1

There's something a little sad about memories wrapped up in newspaper—the wrapping makes them seem less than what they really are.

Mildred Jackson had lived in the same house her entire married life. Three children, a husband, several horses, and twice remodeling and adding on had made a mark on the family homestead that simply couldn't be moved. But the children had left town years before, her arthritic back made it harder and harder to take care of the horses, and her husband, Jim, had passed on the year before.

Mildred knew it was time to move on. Closer to town. Something easier to keep up.

She and her cousin Caleb had made a good start packing that day. She worked in the house while he climbed up into the carport attic to clear it out. The hours sped by, and Joyce, Caleb's wife, phoned to say she had a good supper ready for the three of them. So it was time to stop for the day. Mildred went outside to the carport and called up to her cousin.

"Just a second," Caleb answered. Mildred looked around, seeing how neatly Caleb had stacked the boxes he'd brought down. He and Jim were just alike—orderly. Though she'd never visited the attic—that had been her husband's domain—she knew that all of those boxes sat up there just as straight and measured as a corn row.

"This beats all I've ever seen," Caleb said as he wrestled down a box, his gray hair matted to his forehead by the sweat of an honest day's work.

He let out a short laugh and cocked his head toward the attic. "Did you know you had two boxes of old Sears catalogs up there?"

"You don't say," she replied as Caleb set down the box and climbed up to bring down the other one.

Mildred pulled open the tucked-in flaps of the box and picked up the first catalog in the stack—Christmas 1958. She started to flip through the pages. But then something else caught her eye. Another box nearby, good-sized and age-worn white in color.

She bent down on one knee and tenderly ran her hand across it.

When Caleb came down from the attic, he saw his cousin kneeling beside one of the boxes. He watched her finger as it traced something, lettering of some sort. A soft sob escaped her lips, and he saw tears roll down her face. He dropped the box of catalogs and took a few quick steps toward her, placing his hand on her shoulder. "Are you okay?" he asked.

"Look here," Mildred said. "Jim's handwriting." She gave a little sniffle, and Caleb took out his handkerchief for her. "If that don't beat all," she said, more to herself than anything else. "I would've thought he'd just throw this thing away."

Caleb read the words on the box.

DO NOT OPEN! DO NOT THROW AWAY!
ALWAYS REMEMBER!
DON'T EVER FORGET!
ALL THAT GLITTERS AIN'T GOLD,
IMPORTANT THINGS CAN'T BE BOUGHT
AND SOLD.

After being lost in thought for a moment, Mildred said, "I know what's in that box." Then she gave Caleb a little smile. "Don't worry about me. I'm okay. Just help this old woman up."

After gently pulling Mildred to her feet, and thinking she might want to talk about the memories this box held, Caleb said, "Well, I want to see what inspired Jim Jackson to poetry." Trying to lighten the mood a little, he teased, "As long as it's not some deep, dark secret."

Mildred stood mulling things over. She pretty much had herself pulled together. Then she looked at the 1958 Christmas catalog again. On the front, her husband had written, "page 54." Slowly, she opened the dusty old catalog. The latest, newest, and best of 1958 passed before her eyes as she turned the pages. Finally she settled on page 54. She let out a little laugh.

"You won't believe what's in this other box," Mildred said. "Wait just a minute, and I'll get some scissors."

She stepped inside for a moment and then came back out, scissors in hand. She made for the box, then hesitated.

"Hey," Caleb said, "if you want to wait and do this later, that's okay. Looks kind of private."

"Oh, I suppose the private of it all ended when Jim died," Mildred said. "Anyway, I know what's in here. And the note was to himself, not to us." And with that, Mildred ran the scissors' sharp tip along the tape and opened the box.

Caleb looked down, open-mouthed. He saw silvery slivers of something densely packed. Mildred picked up the Christmas catalog where she had left it. "See, on page 54."

Caleb saw aluminum Christmas trees lighting up the page. There were three of them—best, good, and, from what Caleb could tell, downright scrawny—all shining with a tinseled gleam. The middle one, both in quality and price, had been circled in pen. Another circle marked an accessory: a kind of light projector connected to a translucent plastic wheel.

"Never knew you had one of those things," Caleb said, an unspoken question in his voice.

"Oh, we had one, but not up for Christmas Day," she replied.

"Got to be a story in there somewhere," Caleb suggested.

"Yes, but it'll keep, least 'til after supper. I know what it's like to have food on the table and folks show up late. Let's get going. We can recollect over coffee after supper. I do get to stay for coffee, don't I?" Mildred only half asked.

"And dessert, if I know Joyce," Caleb replied. "C'mon, then, let's get on."

"Alrighty, then," Mildred replied, picking up the 1958

Sears catalogs to take with her—not just Christmas, but the Fall/Winter edition as well.

"Well, hey, Mildred." Joyce Smith hugged her warmly. "How'd the packing go today?"

"Made a good start," Mildred said. "That husband of yours can put in a decent day's work when someone sets him to it."

"Worked hard enough to be hungry, despite the insults," Caleb rejoined with a smile.

So they all sat down to a country supper. Caleb looked over the dining table, steam rising off mashed potatoes, green beans, fried chicken, and cornbread. He held out his hands, one to his wife and the other to his cousin. With head bowed, he prayed, "For mercy everlasting, O Lord, we're thankful. Amen."

It was a short prayer, but heartfelt and powerful. When Caleb and Mildred ate at their granny's table when they were children, it was the prayer that their granny often prayed. Caleb, even as a child, heard those few words and realized a whole life's meaning stood behind them. So he often said the same prayer now, seeing as how so much of who he was came from his granny.

After everyone had taken a few bites, Joyce asked Mildred, "When do you expect the kids?"

"Oh, the weekend. Two more days like today, and we should have everything ready." A sigh slipped past Mildred's lips.

"You sure you're up for this, honey?" Joyce asked as she reached over and squeezed Mildred's hand.

"Oh, I think so—though I hate to leave Smoky Hollow. I loved coming out here when Granny was alive—it was my second home. Always jealous of Caleb for the good life he lived out here in the country." She sighed again. "Well, I got my spell of it, didn't I? A town girl growing up and growing old, a country girl in the middle. Not a bad thing, really."

Joyce patted Mildred's hand.

"Worst of it's been done, anyway," Mildred went on. "Found a place for the last of the horses last week. Should've done it some time ago, I guess, when I got where I couldn't ride much. Still, I liked having 'em around. Watching 'em go has been about as bad as the children leaving home."

"Worse, seems to me," Caleb said. "I always thought you treated those horses better'n your kids."

"Oh, I did not!" Mildred reached over and gently slapped Caleb's arm. "But I did love them. That's part of what made being out here so nice, having horses. Mamma always said I was tetched in the head for wanting the trouble of it." She paused a second. "Course, when you love something, usually it's not as much trouble as seems to other folks."

They ate in silence for a bit, each with thoughts of growing up and growing old and moving on. The thought that ran through all their heads at some point was how fast it all seemed to have gone, that time between the growing up and growing old.

"Well," Joyce finally asked, "you left any room for dessert? I fried some apple pies, and we've got ice cream to go with it."

"That'd be fine," Mildred said.

"How about a bit of coffee to wash it down?" Caleb asked.

"Sure," Mildred replied. "It'll be nice while we talk."

Joyce served up the pies and ice cream while Caleb started coffee. Then he said, "Mildred's brought us books and a story. We can look at the books while the coffee finishes, then we can all sit back and hear a good story."

"Don't know that it's a good story, but maybe an interesting one. And packing up the house has put me in the mood to reminisce." Mildred retrieved the Sears catalogs from where she had put them when she first came in. She sat back down at the table and thumbed through one of the thick books.

"You know," she said, "Jim's mamma used to say there were only two books in the world worth reading—the Bible and the Sears catalog." Mildred laughed. "Being a schoolteacher, I didn't ever know quite how to take that."

"Well, judging by the boxes I brought down, Jim must have loved the Sears catalog, too," Caleb said.

"What do you mean?" Joyce asked.

"You wouldn't believe!" Caleb exclaimed. "Brought down two boxes of nothing but catalogs."

"Time was, early in our marriage," Mildred said, turning a page, "when Jim would stare at one of these things for hours, going on about what the world 'out there' was all about and how he was gonna make it big and move out into that world, buying up all the things he saw in the catalog." Mildred sat and gazed at the pages.

Caleb got up to get the coffee. He knew enough about stories not to interrupt with questions that didn't need to be answered yet. There's storytelling and story listening, and Caleb and Joyce both knew to listen to the story as it was told, throwing out the occasional comment to help grease it along. But that would come later. Caleb poured everyone a cup of coffee.

He watched Mildred as she brought the cup to her lips, giving a quick puff and taking a big sip, daring the coffee to burn her lips. In certain ways, Caleb thought, Mildred stood as the spitting image of her mamma—a straight talker and a straight shooter. A touch of gentleness came to her from her granny, and the result was a woman who spoke her mind yet knew, in certain situations, that the "what for" she wanted to give someone might best be kept to herself at the moment. After all these years, the cousin he grew up with was still one of his favorite people.

Mildred started her story by pointing to the date on the catalog. "If you recall, 1958 was when you two were still living down in Augusta," she said.

"About halfway through medical school," Caleb said. "Real busy. Baby on the way. Didn't get up this way any that year."

"That was a bad year, in a way, for Jim and me," Mildred continued. "The only bad year we really ever had."

Caleb and Joyce sat still, listening.

"Threatened to kick him out," Mildred said, a short snort coming out. "Can you imagine that—me and Jim not being together? That's how bad it got." She ran her hand across the Sears catalog. "Some women got to worry about their man straying. I had to worry about a catalog. And it wasn't the underwear section, either." Mildred laughed again, all of them knowing it wasn't just the young boys who liked to turn to the ladies' underwear pages.

"Those days, Jim got to where he figured the road to happiness was paved with pages from the Sears catalog," Mildred went on. "He wanted everything he saw in there. Thought having stuff made you somebody, and Jim wanted to be somebody so badly he couldn't stand it."

"Well, he ended up pretty well, didn't he? Once he got in the apple business," Joyce said.

Mildred nodded. "We did all right, I guess. Got the kids through school. And better than that, Jim said, was always having a place for them to work. Kept them out of trouble."

Mildred took a sip of coffee. "It wasn't just the kids, though. Something about that orchard worked wonders for Jim. His own place, running things his way. Made him feel worthwhile. Jim was a good man," Mildred said emphatically. "He just needed something to help him remember that. And me giving him a good swift kick on occasion." They all laughed. The image of Mildred actually kicking Jim Jackson, him a good foot taller than she was and retaining most of his life the athletic body of his youth, was something they relished—all the more so because, if Mildred thought it needed to be done, she'd have done it.

"Jim just had to quit running from himself long enough to get a good idea of what he was really made of," Mildred said. "But for six months or so he ran like crazy, hoping to be a big business whiz with offices everywhere except in Gilmer County."

"Suppose all that business with his daddy embarrassed him a bit?" Joyce offered.

"Oh, a little, for a while. But I once told him, there's good and bad with every family. Find out what's good and hold on to it; change the bad, and if you can't, try your best to overlook it; and try to raise your young'uns a little better than you were. That's all anybody can do."

"Still," Caleb allowed, "given the kind of life Jim thought he was going to have, coming back to Smoky Hollow must have been hard."

"It was," Mildred answered. "And it didn't help that Mamma would lay into him every time he tried to talk about the glory days. She'd tell him, 'The past is past, the future ain't got here yet, so just be glad for what you got.' Sometimes Mamma's advice didn't sit well with Jim."

"You don't say!" Caleb let out, and they all laughed. Lois Holt's advice was a little hard for anyone to take. Caleb had been on the wrong side of his aunt Lois's "plain sense" advice too many times to let the comment pass.

"Well, whatever else you can say about it, Jim's folks left all the young'uns plenty of land—at least that didn't get taken away," Joyce said. "Just glad Jim had the sense to get into apples when he did. And now look," Joyce went on, a teasing tone to her voice, "the sale of one of the premier apple orchards in the county has set you up to live a life of luxury in the big city."

Mildred just shook her head and smiled. She took another drink of coffee, pondering a bit about life and her husband and what life might hold now.

"You know," she said, "Mamma was right that the past is past. But sometimes there's teeth in the memories of what's gone before…."

Chapter 2

Little Jimmy played hard. He sat in red clay, his five-year-old body dusty from head to foot. "Rrrrrr," he said as he whipped his little die-cast Ford car around the pretend racetrack, a little oval scraped into the dirt.

"Go, Junior, go!" the little boy let out a holler. He set the car up slightly on its back wheels as it sped down the straightaway.

Jimmy made the sounds a little louder as the yelling increased in the house. He had cleared out, as usual, once his mamma and daddy started in on each other. And even though a little pang of hunger nipped at Jimmy's tummy, he knew to wait until there was less noise inside.

Suddenly the screen door flew open, and Jimmy's daddy stormed out. The sun nicked the top of the mountains now, so Jimmy knew it was time for his daddy to go to work. His daddy was a driver. Sometimes Jimmy got to go driving with his daddy, but not usually when it was work. Jimmy knew that his daddy worked for some farmers in the area because his daddy had told him he drove corn down to Atlanta for them. His daddy always said he had to be careful, though, because the corn he carried came in a jar. Then he'd laugh.

Little Jimmy knew his daddy could drive good, too, because he'd been to Atlanta with his mamma and seen him race. His daddy had explained to him that lots of boys from up in the mountains drove their jars of corn into Atlanta on Saturday night, then all of them hung around so they could race against each other the next day. All the corn drivers needed to be able to drive real fast, Jimmy's daddy had told him. And so Jimmy had heard all the yells of "Go, Junior, go!" That's how he knew how to make his track and what to yell.

Jimmy jumped up and ran after his daddy. Racing around his track had set him in the mood to go riding. With a five-year-old's optimism, he called out, "Hey, Daddy! Let me come!"

Jimmy would always remember that day. Even as an adult, for no reason, he'd have the image pop into his head. In slow motion, he'd see his daddy turn around, face red with rage. That's the day caution caught up with optimism in his little-boy mind.

Jimmy saw his daddy scan the ground, eyes lighting on the little Coca-Cola truck near his feet. One late Sunday night, after a good race, Jimmy's daddy had come home with a present for him. It was the little 1933 Ford truck, painted red, the "Coca-Cola" logo stamped on the door. Daddy had been to someplace called "Woolworth's" on one of his trips and bought it special for him.

Jimmy watched as his daddy picked up the truck. That was his whole collection in the world—that and the Ford car he raced around his little red-clay track.

The surprise, rather than the physical hurt of it, took little Jimmy's breath away. He watched as his daddy wound up and threw the truck like a baseball, right at him, yelling, "Git away from me, boy!" His daddy then got into his car and tore off.

The tears came slowly at first. The truck had struck Jimmy's shoulder a glancing blow. He rubbed the spot; it stung.

Then Jimmy turned toward the house, and he went to where his truck had hit the wall. The tears came quickly then.

"Oh, no!" the little boy cried. "My truck! Oh, no! NO!" The driver's-side door hung crooked—broken.

Jimmy cried until his mamma came out. He told her what had happened, and she tried to comfort him as best she could. Jimmy listened as she said his daddy didn't always mean the things he did; that's just the way he was. He took her hand when she offered it and followed her inside. And then for a while—before the other littl'uns and supper called for his mamma's attention—he had her all to himself. She pulled out their dog-eared Sears catalog, and they flipped through it together. She showed him the kinds of things she'd like to have and let him point out some of the toys he'd like. But when he asked her if she could get a new toy truck for him, she just looked down with sad eyes. "We ain't got no money for that, son."

And then, almost as an afterthought, as if saying it more to herself than to her boy, she added, "We're the kind of folks that mostly gets to look."

Jimmy stood a couple of aisles over in the store, eavesdropping on what his daddy was saying to some customers who had just walked in. He knew his daddy was standing behind the cash register, leafing through a copy of the *Times-Courier.*

"See my boy in the paper?" Junior Jackson asked his customers. Jimmy heard the rattling of newsprint, and he knew his daddy was holding up the paper, showing off the front-page picture of Jimmy all dressed up in his football uniform. The headline proclaimed, "Ellijay Football Star Accepts Scholarship to the University of Georgia."

Jimmy felt a little surge of satisfaction, thinking about that scholarship offer and all that had led up to it. The Ellijay team hadn't won the state championship that year, but they'd come close, with Jimmy commanding the team like a general. He'd quarterbacked and run the ball a lot. But his kicking was what had brought in the crowds, even out-of-towners.

It started back when he was a junior, first game of the season. Everyone stood up to watch the kickoff, then a collective gasp of surprise escaped from the crowd as Jimmy's kickoff soared through the air, higher than anyone had ever seen. At first, people who hadn't been at the game couldn't believe what the paper said: "Ellijay Kicker Boots One Through the Goalposts." As far as anyone could remember, it was the first time anyone had stood at his own forty-yard line and put the ball over the goalposts at the other end. And it wasn't the last.

Jimmy knew his daddy liked the attention, being the father of a star. He often heard his daddy bragging on him to the customers, though his daddy never said a word to him about it. His daddy kept on treating him the way he always had—like a young'un without a lick of sense who needed to be whipped just for the good of it. Still, Jimmy felt good when he heard snippets here and there about how Junior stood proud of his boy.

He was glad, too, that his family had the store now. He'd listened through the screen door one night and heard his mamma and daddy out on the front porch swing, talking about how their lives had changed the past few years. Jimmy heard his daddy tell his mamma how she'd been right after all. She'd been the one who talked him into giving up his whiskey runs and buying the general store in Ellijay. They talked about how the regular customers made his living and his special customers made it a good living. They were the ones to whom he sold those hundred-pound sacks of sugar. Moonshining required a lot of sugar added to corn to make the corn mash. But *selling* the sugar—that was perfectly legit, he figured. All up-front and respectable—and profitable. Little by little, with the money those big sacks of sugar brought in, Junior had been buying up land in Smoky Hollow, where the family lived.

Now, ten years into business, Junior Jackson considered himself the all-American success story. The son doing well was icing on the cake. Listening at the door that night, Jimmy had heard his daddy laugh and say, "And I like cake."

Jimmy's attention snapped back to the present. He heard his daddy's customers saying they needed some sugar to sweeten their corn. Jimmy knew then what kind of customers they were.

"Let me go and find my boy," Junior said, putting the paper down. "Come on around back, and we'll load you up."

Junior took off for the back of the store, and the moonshiners slammed the door on the way to get their truck. Jimmy started to follow his dad but had only taken a couple of steps when he heard a couple of women talking. They must have come into the store while his daddy was talking to the 'shiners.

"Listen to him, talkin' like he's somebody," one woman said. "He ain't no better'n the ones he sells that sugar to. A nobody from nowhere, just like the rest of 'em."

"Ain't that right," the other woman replied. Jimmy thought he recognized her voice—a regular customer. "He's got him a store, but he's still a 'shiner at heart, making his living off the 'shiners. And that boy—" the woman's voice dripped with disapproval "—Don't you know he's gonna turn out just as worthless as his old man. All that talk about football and goin' off to college, but you wait and see if'n he don't end up back here, a drunk like his old man."

"The apple don't fall far from the tree, does it?" the one said.

"Ain't it the truth," replied the other, "and in this case, the tree's just plain rotten to the core. Now, let's see. I need me some of that White Lily flour...."

Red in the face, Jimmy hurried to the back of the store, skirting the aisles to avoid the two gossiping women. For just a second, he thought about telling his daddy what he'd just heard. But then, as soon as his daddy saw him, he said, "Where you been, boy? There's some sugar needs loading up."

Jimmy's mouth hung open, about to speak, but nothing came out.

"Get a move on," his daddy snapped, "and don't stand there like a danged idjit that's worthless as a lump on a log. I want to close up and get on home."

By that time, the truck had backed up to the little makeshift loading dock. Jimmy grabbed a hundred-pound sack of sugar and flung it into the truck a lot harder than necessary.

"I know it got to Jim, the way some people talked," Mildred said, setting down her empty cup, "though it was really just a few ol' biddies in town. Most folks—you know how it was—saw running 'shine as just another way to get by. Weren't that many ways to make a living back there in the mountains. And they certainly didn't blame Jim for the way his daddy was."

"Course, it didn't hurt that he was a football star," said Caleb.

Mildred smiled. "Or that he was smart and hand-some. You remember—half the girls at school were in love with him."

"Including you?" Joyce teased.

"Not me," she answered. "Not yet. I mean, I liked him—hard not to like Jim. And we said hey to each other in the halls or down at his daddy's store. But, you know how it is in high school; everybody has their own little crowd. Me and Jim ran in different circles—him with the good-looking ones, me with Caleb and his crowd."

"Hey," Caleb threw in, "I practically defined the good-looking crowd."

Joyce laughed and gave her husband an affection-ate smile. "Best-looking redhead, anyway," she said.

"But Mildred, you and Jim both went to college down at Georgia. Didn't you run into him there?"

"Once or twice. But he was a BMOC there, too—you know, a big man on campus. And he always seemed to have a girlfriend, so I never expected him to pay much attention to me."

"Besides," she said, "I always liked it here at home, and Jim knew I was coming back here when I finished. And Jim—" she smiled ruefully and shook her head "—Jim had big plans."

She shook her head a little sadly. "Once Jim Jackson left Smoky Hollow behind, he had no intentions of ever coming back."

Chapter 3

Jimmy grinned as he held up a copy of *The Red and Black*. The University of Georgia student newspaper carried a picture of his game-winning kick against Georgia Tech. And that's what Jimmy loved best about being a college football star. Of course, he liked the games themselves and the way everyone picked him up after one of his kicks lifted Georgia over its rivals. But seeing his picture in the paper and knowing that people all over campus were seeing it, too—that was the best.

He'd been in the paper more than he had a right to expect, in some ways. He hadn't started at quarterback his freshman year, and he hadn't started his sophomore year, either. But he'd worked hard at it, and he had hopes that he'd be the starter his junior year. And even without starting at the quarterback position, he'd had his share of pictures, because everyone knew that Jimmy Jackson had been *the* University of Georgia placekicker from the moment he stepped onto campus.

Sometimes he'd sit in his dorm room and look at the

scrapbook he'd begun back in high school—already the college articles outnumbered earlier ones. Then he'd pull down the *Pandora* from his freshman year. He'd flip quickly through the college yearbook until he hit the football section. There he stood, famous in a black-and-white photo. No one in his family had ever had a picture in a book like this.

That picture meant he wasn't a nobody moonshine runner's boy. Meant he was somebody.

And he felt like somebody today. Picture in the paper again. Grades okay. A girl from Monticello—a cheerleader—was sweet on him. He'd see her later, just like he'd seen her the night before, celebrating after the big victory. Most of the players liked him, and almost everybody respected and admired him. A couple of them harbored some jealousy, but he thought that was only natural. Talk about him being a professional football player took the shine off a few of the seniors who thought they ought to be in the spotlight. Still, winning was winning, and he'd had a big hand in it—or a big foot—especially if the games were close.

Jimmy put down the paper and started out to meet his buddies at The Grill. They'd throw back a few burgers, talk more about the game, and then spend some time with their sweeties. What a life! And Jimmy knew it'd just get better. Living at the university in Athens sure beat the fire out of Smoky Hollow and Ellijay, but joining a pro team would mean moving on to a big city. New York. Chicago. St. Louis. Cleveland. And Jimmy wanted to be someplace big enough that he could be a whole new him, not just some 'shine runner's boy who'd made good. He wanted people to look up to him, to see what he could do and what he could be—not just a hometown star or even a college one, but a real success out in the world. This football thing was opening doors he meant to walk through and then slam shut.

As his thoughts wandered, Jimmy nearly ran over a young woman on the sidewalk. After they had gotten out their *pardon me*'s, he caught a look at her face. And smiled.

"Well, hey, Mildred," Jimmy said.

Mildred Holt looked up and gave him a broad grin. "Don't you know 'hey' is for horses and cows?"

It took a second for that to sink in with Jimmy. He laughed, but too late to pretend he'd gotten the joke right away.

"You that quick in class?" Mildred asked with a grin.

"Naw," Jimmy said. "Hey…" he started, then laughed again. "Listen," he began over. "I'm going over to The Grill to meet some of the boys from the team. Wanna come?"

Jimmy had always liked Mildred. She lived in Elli-jay, but she had visited in Smoky Hollow quite a bit. Her granny had lived there, and her family still went to the church in the Hollow where Jimmy's family went for funerals and such. And of course he knew her from high school, being as there was only one high school in the whole county. At one time, it had been called the Ellijay Academy, but now it was known as Gilmer High School.

Mildred had always been nice to him, and she had a feisty way about her that drew him to her but made him a little afraid of her, too. He knew that no one back in high school ever wanted to get into a verbal sparring with Mildred. It was said that Mildred took after her mamma, Lois: if need be, she could peel paint off the wall with her words.

"Thanks, Jimmy, but I'd better not." Mildred said. "Got too much homework to do." Jimmy knew Mildred attended Georgia so that she could be a teacher. She could have done it somewhere else cheaper, but Mildred's mamma wanted the best for Mildred. "This is my first semester, and I want to do well," Mildred added.

"Okay," Jimmy said, a little disappointed. "All the studying's kinda hard getting used to, isn't it?" Jimmy wished he could have taken the words back as soon as he said them. Someone as smart as Mildred probably didn't have problems doing the work. He'd meant to sound like the consoling, older friend who'd been there a whole year longer and knew what she was going through. But maybe he'd just sounded dumb.

"Oh, it's not so bad," Mildred replied. "Probably not as hard as what you're doing." Mildred knew that Jimmy planned to major in business administration—a popular choice among the football players.

"I do all right," Jimmy said, trying to sound breezy. Actually, between football practice and socializing, Jimmy didn't have as much time as he needed to study, but he got by.

"See you later, then," Mildred said.

"Later," Jimmy replied as she walked off, sorry to see her go.

Jimmy made it to The Grill and spotted the gang. He sat down next to Max Nelson. Max always talked about his hometown of Macon as if it were the crown jewel of the southern cities. Max had once asked Jimmy, "Why don't you ever tell stories about Ellijay, or whatever they call that place you're from?" Jimmy once, only once, had tried to tell his friends the difference between where he went to school—Ellijay—and where his home was—Smoky Hollow. By the time everyone let him know what a lot of trouble that distinction was to make, he had let it drop. "Don't have any stories," Jimmy had told Max, "except for ones about footballs sprouting wings and flying over goalposts."

"A story that goes on," Max had said, slapping Jimmy's back.

"Reckon it does," Jimmy had agreed.

A big defensive lineman named Bill Miller leaned across the table, liquor on his breath, and said, "We're getting ready for a big night." He brought a brown paper sack out from under the table and pushed it in Jimmy's direction. "Now, how would that economics professor of ours say it? 'Care to partake of these libations?'"

Jimmy laughed along with everyone else and slowly—but insistently—pushed the bottle away. "Naw, don't drink baby stuff," he said. "Only thing strong enough for us mountain boys comes from a Mason jar."

They all laughed, and the conversation and drinking moved on—which is what Jimmy intended. He made a pretense of only liking corn mash—grew up with it since a baby, he'd say, nursing from a bottle. But the fact of the matter was, Jimmy didn't drink. So he spent the next couple of hours watching two or three of his friends getting drunker than skunks, as they put it. But they weren't mean drunks, just funny ones. And they entertained the rest of them, although the ones who had had at least some to drink found the drunks funnier than Jimmy did.

Still, these were his friends, and this was his team, and these guys were his ticket to where he was going. So, when it came time to go, Jimmy didn't resent having to steady one or two of them as they made their way out the door and down the street.

The crowd spilled out of The Grill. "Bulldogs on the loose!" yelled Bill Miller, a dopey smile plastered on his face. He'd had a good meal, drunk too much, and stepped out into the cool evening air that carried a promise of romance. "The girls love football players," he said. "And I'm one of the big ones!"

They walked two or three together on their way to the girls' dorm. Jimmy walked between Bill and Max the way he usually did. "These are my fellers," he'd tell people. "The heart of the line. If they don't keep 'em out, the ball doesn't go flying over." Bill and Max always liked the attention Jimmy's words brought to them, so Jimmy had gained two bruisers for friends. They always made a point of taking care of "their" kicker.

As they swaggered down the street, Bill bumped into Jimmy, who bumped into Max. "Sorry, man," Bill started. But then Max, seeing a game, bumped Jimmy back into Bill. "Ping-Pong!" Max yelled.

Max and Bill good naturedly bumped Jimmy back and forth between them, laughing their heads off partly because the two of them held enough liquor to put four or five smaller men under, but also because they just wanted to laugh and have fun. Jimmy laughed, too, and he hadn't had a drop.

But fun quickly turned to disaster. Bill bumped Jimmy hard, bellowing out "Point!" like he really was playing Ping-Pong and had just slammed the ball. Max tripped over his own feet and fell the slow fall of a big drunk guy. The force of Bill's Ping-Pong smash sent Jimmy hurtling toward Max, while Max's fall put the big man's body at about Jimmy's knees. Jimmy somersaulted, just as if he'd taken a big hit on the field, and landed in the street, the breath knocked out of him. The force of the blow had flipped him around so that he lay on his stomach, head near the curb and legs sprawled out in the middle of the road.

A horn blowing, the sound of rubber screeching, and the realization that there were cars on the road caused Jimmy to start to move. He brought his left leg up to push off. But then time ran out.

The driver tried to swerve, but the brakes locked and the back driver's-side wheel refused to turn. It skidded over Jimmy's right foot, smashing the bones from ankle to toes. And in a matter of seconds—seconds marred by a mix of buddies joshing and tragic coincidences—the gridiron star from Ellijay became just the boy from Smoky Hollow—a boy who used to set footballs to flight but now mostly limped along.

"The school paid the medical bills," Mildred said, "and the scholarship paid for the rest of the school year. Of course, I didn't know that until a lot later. I just heard about the accident, and it sounded awful, but that was about all."

"But Jim stayed in school, at least for a little while, didn't he?" asked Caleb. "I remember that. Must have felt like a comedown, having to give up football."

"Well, he missed being on the team, but he figured if he buckled down and did well at school, he could still get a decent job in business administration. He remained as upbeat as a person could be after a blow like that—he just figured his ticket out had changed, that's all. And he was pretty sure his daddy could help keep him in school, especially if Jim worked a couple of jobs in the summer—at the store and logging and maybe second shift at the sock mill. He was absolutely determined to keep on the path he'd chosen. But then it seemed that one thing happened after another, and all Jim's plans had to change."

When the call came in on the dormitory phone that spring, the end of his sophomore year, Jimmy had his books spread out to study, but he'd mostly been sitting there planning, dreaming up ways to make money for school after his scholarship ran out.

"Phone for you, Jimmy," some guy from Epworth told him. Since he'd been on the team, most everybody knew Jimmy, and he liked that. And he was a decent enough human being to feel sorry that he didn't know the name of the kid who called him to the phone.

Jimmy walked out into the hall to take the call. He talked on the phone a little while. And after he hung up, everything seemed normal enough. He walked back to his room and sat back down at his desk. The lights stayed on, the quiet of the room kept its quiet.

And that's the way of it, most of the time. A man's

world falls in around him, and for a minute or two, during the shock of it all, he expects there to be great crashing sounds, like the earth being torn asunder beneath his very feet. He expects the lights to all go out, and he waits for darkness to settle in over the whole world.

But none of that happened the day Jimmy's world fell apart. Almost never does. So, after waiting a respectful spell to see if it would come to pass, Jimmy went back to studying—as good a way to see it through as any. He'd never have guessed so few words said over a telephone could be so devastating.

"It's terrible, Jimmy. You've got to come home...."

Chapter 4

"The family tragedy brought us together," Mildred said. "I mean the last one involving Jim's daddy," she added, nodding her head to say "whoa" as Caleb refilled her coffee cup.

"How'd that bring you together?" Caleb asked.

"Well," Mildred said, "Jim's daddy passed away in 1953." They all sat in silence a moment, remembering the questionable circumstances that had led to Junior Jackson's death.

"I'd been out of college about a year, teaching at Harmony school," Mildred continued. "Of course, Jim had been back home a few years then, trying to hold things together for the family after his daddy got arrested. Then his daddy died in prison, and the preacher asked me to sing at the funeral—along with your daddy, Caleb.

"Funny place to hit things off," she mused, "but it all got started at that funeral."

My latest sun is sinking fast,
My race is nearly run;

My strongest trials now are past,
My triumph is begun.
O come, angel band,
Come and around me stand;
O bear me away on your snowy wings
To my immortal home.

Robert Smith strummed the guitar, a callused thumb
evoking just the right tone. His high tenor voice, trembling with emotion, brought tears to Jimmy's eyes. But
his eyes stayed open, because he was also noticing for
the first time what a pretty girl Mildred Holt was. She
and her uncle Robert sang at a lot of funerals in the
area—if you could be famous for good funeral singing,
then they were about as famous as you could get. He
knew they even sang out of the county on occasion.

Jimmy wondered now if he should've tried to court
Mildred rather than the fair-weather girlfriends at Georgia who'd left him the minute he was no longer a star.
After his accident, he'd figured himself to be pretty
much the same person, but not too many people from his
crowd down in Athens had. He'd gotten tossed aside like
an old toy truck, and hard enough that he felt broken—
wrong. Like he'd never been good enough.

The second verse caught Jimmy's attention.

O, bear my longing heart to him
Who bled and died for me;
Whose blood now cleanses from all sin,
And gives me victory.

Victory—that's what I need, Jimmy thought. *A win
with a capital* W, *something to change my life.* But

given all that had happened, all that was going on, he couldn't think how that was going to come about. His mind kept wandering after questions of what would come next, whether he'd ever manage to escape this place that seemed to keep pulling him back. But thinking that way didn't seem right, not with his daddy dead and all. So he focused his eyes and attention on Mildred, hearing her alto voice give foundation to Mr. Smith's flight of emotion.

Preacher Wingate stood up. He'd been preaching at Smoky Hollow Church going on five years. The old preacher before him, Buford Lattimer, had preached literally until his dying day. He'd had a heart attack right in the middle of a Sunday morning message—seventy-three years old and still blistering the pulpit, calling sinners home. Preacher Wingate had been converted under the old man, came to recognize his call to preach during a revival Preacher Lattimer had led, and preached his first sermon under his tutelage.

Preacher Wingate was a true disciple of the only preacher he had known growing up. So he carried on in the old pulpiteer's tradition, which meant, on this occasion, using the funeral service as a reminder of the dangers of hell. Preacher Wingate wanted to give everybody a chance to repent before the next performance of a casket being carried out of the church.

"Victory!" Preacher Wingate slammed the pulpit with his fist. "That's what needs to be talked about at a time like this."

Jimmy listened to Preacher Wingate. Normally, he'd tune him out at funerals, because he always seemed to say the same thing. But this time the preacher echoed Jimmy's own thoughts, so he listened.

Funerals like these were really the only times Jimmy had been to church. His wasn't a churchgoing family, for the most part. His mamma had always gone as a child and sometimes talked about going back. But with Junior working on most Sundays and not much interested in church to start with, she'd found it easier to stay home, and even with Junior gone, she had a hard time picking up the churchgoing habit again. Like everyone else, they had a family Bible, and Jimmy's mamma would read from it now and again, mostly when Junior was out for the night working. Jimmy remembered snuggling up against his mother on those nights as she read stories from that big old Bible.

Preacher Wingate was speaking now about how it was Christ that won victory on the cross. Jimmy had heard that before, of course. He even believed it, insofar as you can believe something without it making much difference. Mountain religion was part of mountain life. Jimmy believed; he just didn't know that it mattered much.

But then Jimmy heard something he hadn't before. Preacher Wingate started in on what happens when somebody gets saved. "Washed clean," Preacher Wingate was shouting. "Clean, I say! Whiter'n snow. That's what blessed Isaiah says. Though your sins be as scarlet, *I,* the Lord your God, will make them white as snow.

"More'n that," he went on. "It's not like you just been dunked in the washer, sins slapped out of you like dirt. No," he said. "You're a brand-new person."

And that's what hooked Jimmy.

"When you get yourself baptized, when you have your sins wiped clean, it's more than just the same old you spiffied up a bit," Preacher Wingate said. "Bible says we become brand-new. New creatures, the blessed apostle Paul says. Listen to him: 'Therefore if any man be in Christ, he is a new creature: old things are passed away; behold, all things are become new.'"

Preacher Wingate said more. "When you get put six feet under," he asked, "do you want it to be as a child of God, or his enemy?" Preacher put the poignancy of it all to them. Death reigned among them. Junior Jackson ran a fast race that ended in a fiery crash—everyone appreciated the racing image. They preferred to have their minds drawn to the picture of Junior out racing rather than Junior sitting in a prison cell, which was where he had died.

"All races end with a crash and a burn," Preacher said. "Thing is, do you want to go out a winner or a loser? I don't know about Junior Jackson. I don't know what was in his heart when his race ended. I don't know what's in your heart either. Only you do. Only you. You going out a winner, made new by God hisself? Or is the crash and burn only the start of an eternity of flame? It's up to you. It's up to you. Listen to your heart. See if God doesn't call you out to be one of the victors that rides the victory lap to the tune of angel bands. Come now. Come now."

Preacher Wingate moved up by the casket, ready to welcome anyone who responded to his message and came to the front to get saved, but not really expecting anyone to do it. He had never had anyone actually step forward at a funeral. He'd only even seen it once or twice, and that when he was a boy. Some churches had stopped doing altar calls altogether at funerals; some said it was better simply to give respect to the dead and comfort the ones left behind than to stir up the family with a lot of hellfire. But Preacher Wingate came from the old school.

The only person more surprised than Preacher Wingate when Jimmy Jackson lurched purposefully down the aisle was Jimmy himself. He leaned to whisper to Preacher and said, "I want it. I want to be a new man." He hadn't meant to walk the aisle, but he had. Preacher's words and his own worries and the haunting sound of Mildred's voice, like it was part of the angel band itself, had moved him.

And once he started walking, his halting steps took on a purpose of their own.

"Jim took his saving seriously—not like some," Mildred said. "After he got baptized, he hit those church steps just about every time the door opened. He was a good man before and a better man after. I mean, he had his faults, but he always tried to do right."

Joyce reached over and patted Mildred's hand.

"Anyway, I still remember being surprised when he walked the aisle at his daddy's funeral. That was…different. I hadn't seen that happen before. And afterward, Uncle Robert and I stood toward the end of the line, everybody shaking Jim's hand, saying how sorry they were because his daddy had passed away, but at the same time congratulating him on being saved. And Jim standing there looking sad and happy and a little confused, all at the same time."

A tear made its way down Mildred's cheek.

"Felt pleased as punch when Jim took my hand, very gently. 'Thank you for the music,' he said. Then he went all sheepish and asked if I'd sing at his baptizing. Said I would be glad to, and after I said it he kept holding my hand. And my goodness, he was a good-lookin' man back then."

Mildred let herself get lost again in thinking about a young man who had held her hand and later held her heart.

"What'd you sing?" Joyce asked.

Mildred smiled. "'What a Friend We Have in Jesus.' Can you believe I still remember that? We went down to the river the next Sunday like we always did, finishing up the service with the baptizing. Jim had wanted me to sing right before he was baptized. So he and Preacher stood there still as statues, up to their waists in the river, while I sang."

Mildred sat outside, rocking on her front porch, thinking about Jimmy. The baptizing had been nice, and she knew she'd done a good job. She mulled over his words, the ones he'd said when he told her what song he wanted sung. And then she thought about the conversation they had afterward, their first really long talk.

"I like the message," Jimmy said as they sat side by side on the church steps. "'What a Friend we have in Jesus, all our sins and griefs to bear.'" Silence passed between them for a few minutes, and awkwardness never interrupted it. Mildred felt comfortable in Jimmy's presence, so she just sat there and eased into it, finding it easy to relax. Then he leaned forward, his chin on his hands. "Guess that's what I've been needing the past few years."

"Must've been hard," she said gently. "What with your dad and having to leave school and all. And…the accident."

He nodded, the shock of black hair on his forehead falling forward the way she remembered seeing it in high school. It was strange to see him here, looking so familiar and yet so different from how she'd always known him.

"Don't reckon I've had it as bad as some," he said. "It's kinda hard to take, though. Seemed like everything was going good, and now everything's changed…."

Mildred leaned her elbows on her knees, her eyes attentive. She figured she'd hear the full story of what had happened to Jimmy and how he'd ended up back in Smoky Hollow. She'd heard bits and pieces, facts mixed up with gossip, but not the heart of it all, the part that lay so heavy on Jimmy's soul. And as she sat next to him, she realized she wanted to hear it all. It was a big step Jimmy was taking, talking to her as if she were that someone special you tell secrets to, and so she listened hard, wanting to be worthy of his trust.

"You probably don't remember," he added, "but I ran into you on campus the same day I…the day the car hit me."

But she did remember. She remembered the electricity running through her when Jimmy Jackson invited her to go to The Grill with him. Made her hair practically curl with excitement. But she also remembered seeing him with a steady girl, with plenty of others lined up to take her place. And Mildred had never been one to stand in line that way. So she'd told him no, even though she had wanted to say yes.

But she didn't tell him that now. She just nodded. "I felt really bad later when I heard about it. Did you get my card?"

He nodded, too. "That was real nice of you. Guess I shoulda called and thanked you. But after I got out of the hospital, I…well, anyway, I shoulda done it."

"You didn't have to," she said softly. "It was just a card."

"Thing is," he added, "that's when everything started to go bad. But I didn't know it then. I just thought it was a little setback, and I'd get through it. Then the next semester I got the news about Daddy going to jail, and I had to come home…."

Jimmy seemed awfully embarrassed about that part, but still he told the full story. When he finished, Mildred reached over and took his hand. And it felt right. She squeezed a little, and she saw a smile flash across a sad face before running back to hide somewhere deep inside.

She wasn't ready to admit it to herself, but she'd give a lot to see that smile again.

"That whole thing was awfully hard on Jim," Mildred said. "He didn't cry or anything when he told it, but you could tell a bone-deep sadness lay on him."

"It all worked out in the end," Caleb offered.

"Yeah, but the shame of it still got to him," Mildred said.

"Plumb foolishness, if you ask me," Joyce said. "I'm not defending the moonshining, but what the revenuers did to Junior Jackson just wasn't right—taking his store like that."

"Well, they thought they had to stop the 'shine running one way or another," Mildred said. "And there was some law about aiding and abetting known criminals, and the government ended up arguing that Junior had to know that what he sold was supplies for moonshining."

"Got him on the bulk, didn't they?" Caleb said. "No regular household comes in and buys hundred-pound sacks of sugar. You think Jim knew what his daddy was doing?"

"Oh he knew, and he hated it. But what was he supposed to do—him just a boy and all?" Mildred asked. "I think the worst part was that Jim thought the actual moonshining part was all in the past, that his daddy had put the illegal part behind him. Then for him to be arrested, and to have the whole moonshining past dredged up again—that was just awful for Jim."

"I still think they could've left the store," Joyce insisted. "After all, there was a family involved."

"'Seizure of property involved in a crime,'" Mildred said, repeating the words told to her by Jim. "So, with Junior in prison and the store gone, Mrs. Jackson didn't have much choice but to call Jim home. She couldn't keep him in school—didn't have the money and didn't have a way to make any. Course, they still had all that land Junior had been buying up, but the reason he could buy it up in the first place was because it wasn't worth anything."

"Couldn't give mountain land away back then," Caleb said.

"No," Mildred replied. "Came in handy later, of

course. But for right then, with Junior locked up, Jim had to come home and help support his family. And later, when Junior died—well, he just had to keep doing it."

"Jim always did right by his family," Caleb said.

"Yes, he did," Mildred said. "And not just his family. I think that's part of what made me fall in love with him. He did right by everyone." She looked over at Caleb. "Remember that time back in high school when you and me met Bobby Ferguson to go to the movies? And there were these three goons from the football team that gave us a hard time?"

"Oh yeah," Caleb acknowledged. "They threw a football at Bobby's leg brace, thinking it funny to knock a feller down who'd had polio."

"Bobby Ferguson," Caleb smiled, recollecting the name of the boy who'd been his best friend while he was growing up in Smoky Hollow. Mildred smiled, too, thinking of her first sweetheart, the boy who had shared her first kiss. And of course Joyce smiled, joining them, all remembering one of the most decent human beings they had ever known.

Mildred laughed. "I still remember trying to scorch their hides with whatever names I could think to call them, knocking down a cripple like that. Then you said something, then Bobby. Then they came toward us, like they were gonna get us."

"I'd have hated to see how that ended," Joyce said.

"But then up comes Jim, out of nowhere," Mildred said. "He said, just as easygoing as you please, 'What you fellers doing?' And then they said, 'Ain't no business of yours, Jimmy.' And then he said, 'That's right, 'cause there ain't no business of any kind going on here, is there, boys?' And the way he came and stood over them, you could see them shrinking right before your eyes. And then, just as polite as can be, he says, 'Why don't we run on to practice and leave these good folks to their movie?'"

"That was a relief, when they left," Caleb admitted.

"A good thing for Jim to do," Mildred said. She let out a girlish giggle. "And as he left, he winked at me."

And they all burst out laughing. When it all subsided, Mildred said again, "Jim was just the kind of fellow that tried to do right."

Chapter 5

Jimmy stood watching over the work at the sawmill. Soon he'd have the logs he'd brought in rough sawn and ready to take to the lumberyard over in Chatsworth. The lumberyard had its own sawmill, too, but Jimmy had found he made a little more if he let these local boys do the first cutting. He'd bring in a good truckload of logs from his family's land, unload them, wait for the cutting, then load all the wood back up and make the trip to Chatsworth.

For quite a while now, he'd been in the habit of working during the week at the carpet mill nearby and logging on Saturday when the weather was nice. It wasn't a lot of money, but it was enough to keep his mamma going—she had no other source of income. Now his two brothers were old enough to help out in a way they couldn't at first. And that was what Jimmy had been waiting for.

Old man Moore came over, more sawdust on top of his head than hair. He took out an old dirty handkerchief and mopped his beet-red face. The day stood hot, and sawmilling made for sweaty, dirty business.

Jimmy pulled out the requisite number of bills and thanked Mr. Moore. The old fellow reached out with a hand that only had two and a half fingers left—hazard of the trade. Jimmy had once expressed sympathy to Mr. Moore about his fingers, and the old man had laughed. "I seen men cut in half doing this," he said. "If I go home not missing anything bigger'n a finger, I count myself a lucky man."

"My brother Harold will be coming in from now on," Jimmy told the sawmill owner. Moore just thumbed through the bills to make sure he'd been paid right.

"Got myself promoted to head of shipping down at Ellijay Carpet," Jimmy continued. "Won't quite have the time I had before."

"Well, then. Thank ye for yore business," the old-timer told Jimmy, turning back toward the contraption with razor-sharp teeth that he and his boys had run for years now.

Jimmy rolled his eyes, annoyed at Mr. Moore's dismissal. He'd just been making conversation. And he'd figured the man would want to know who'd be bringing in the logs from now on.

Doesn't know who he's dealing with, don't guess, Jimmy thought as he walked back toward his old, rattle-trap truck. *Probably never has known who's who, stuck back up this far in the woods. Heck, probably don't know what in the world a head of shipping is, anyway.*

Jimmy coaxed the truck to life and drove away. Usually, he managed to keep down his feelings about being stuck in Smoky Hollow, doing work he didn't care for, feeling obligated to take care of his mother and brothers when all he really wanted was to get away. But those emotions rumbled under the surface; he could feel them throbbing in his veins. He even felt that way today, though the knowledge that he wasn't going logging anymore helped a lot.

If anybody had seen him at the time, they would've sworn they'd just seen a man who was grimacing and grinning at the same time.

"Jim's promotion to head of shipping was a pretty big break for us," Mildred said. "But it was the next promotion that got us in trouble."

"Started out at the mill when it opened, didn't he?" Caleb asked.

"Yep," Mildred replied. "He'd been there from the start. The Nordwalls, they came down from Illinois about '53 and opened up the carpet mill. Jim and I had just married. Seemed a good deal. Jimmy made fairly decent money, and I kept on teaching school for a couple of years before Johnny was born. It's back then that we decided to put what extra money we had into planting a few apple trees in the areas Jim had cleared by logging. Not much of an orchard back then, just enough for us to eat and put some up for apple pie in the winter, plus some to give to family."

"We got along pretty well," Mildred went on. "Never did fight much—not like some couples who live from one fight to the next. And Jim was ready to turn the logging business over to his younger brothers—they were old enough to do a decent job of it by then. So he gave 'em a good talking-to, said they were the ones still living at home—not married, no family yet, so they needed to be men and take up responsibility. We'd help out, too, of course, but they had to do their share." Mildred grinned. "Course, he got all that from me."

"No doubt," Caleb said.

"So, anyway, things stood good between us. By '58, Johnny was three. Rachel had just started walking—a little over a year old—and of course Sarah hadn't been born yet."

Mildred paused. "Then Jim got promoted again, and something that should've been good seemed to bring out something in him that I just couldn't abide."

Mildred blew out a big sigh. "Only really rough spot in our whole married life. Looking back, I'm surprised we got through it at all."

Jimmy sat uneasily in Mr. Nordwall's office. He held tightly to the cup of coffee he had just been offered.

"Ever been outside Gilmer County?" Mr. Nordwall asked, well aware that Jimmy had been down in Athens as a football player.

"For a couple of years," Jimmy replied. "I played football for the Georgia Bulldogs."

"That right?" Nordwall asked, but it was not really a question because he already knew it.

"I've been all around," Nordwall continued. "From Illinois, you know. Decatur. Ever heard of Decatur, Illinois?"

"No, sir, don't think I have," Jimmy replied.

"Nice place. Midwest is a lot like the South, you know," Mr. Nordwall went on. "A lot of hardworking people—but they've been ruined by the unions. There's a lot of companies up there now just about shut down by the unions. The people would work maybe if the union would let them."

This seemed to be a sore spot for Mr. Nordwall.

"Now, of course, I think the worst place is up in the Northeast," Mr. Nordwall continued, a sour look on his face. "I lived there for a year or so, in Massachusetts. My father sent me there to learn the carpet business."

Jimmy squirmed in his chair. He didn't know if the silence that followed signaled a time for him to speak up or if Mr. Nordwall was just reminiscing about his time around Boston. Jimmy knew that Nordwall had spent time around Boston somewhere, though not right in the city. Jimmy had always wanted to go to Boston, a big place with a big history. He knew that from his course in American history down in Athens.

"Anyway," Mr. Nordwall finally continued.

"Ah, yes sir," Jimmy let out.

"Yes sir, what?" Nordwall asked, then caught himself. "Oh, I see. Just agreeing with me about my father sending me off to learn the business." Jimmy thought maybe Mr. Nordwall wasn't much used to small talk, or the little phrases people threw in to kind of slide the conversation in the direction it was meant to go.

"Anyway," Mr. Nordwall finally continued, "you'd think all the people living up there had hung the moon just because they were born in Massachusetts. Now me, I don't see what's so special about it all. So they're descended from a bunch of Pilgrims blown up on shore three hundred years ago. Big deal."

Jimmy thought Mr. Nordwall sounded awfully bitter about his time in Massachusetts.

"But I did learn something important up there," Nordwall went on. "I learned that the carpet business in the Northeast is on its last legs. Unions have ruined them."

Mr. Nordwall paused again, but this time Jimmy figured the conversation would go on just as well if he kept his mouth shut.

"This'll be the place," Mr. Nordwall declared. "My father and I have seen the future of carpet, and it's here in North Georgia. Right here. We're running plants the way they should be run," Nordwall said, giving Jimmy the nod that it was okay to agree with him.

"Yes sir," Jimmy acknowledged, "seems to work good here."

"I oversee this operation, my brother in Dalton manages a couple others, and my father's financing it all from back home." Mr. Nordwall shook his head now as if agreeing with himself, as if to say that his father had had a very fine idea, getting into the new carpet industry in the South.

Then Mr. Nordwall leaned slightly toward Jimmy, taking on an air that there existed between himself and Jimmy a certain level, if not of intimacy, then of shared confidence.

"It'll be people like you and me that builds the carpet empire," Mr. Nordwall said, looking hard at Jimmy for some sign of reaction.

Mr. Nordwall waited a second, feeling for a response, then went on. "You and me, Jimmy. Do you hear what I'm saying? I've seen your work. I've seen the way you supervise people. You're a born manager, son, a born manager."

Jimmy sat a little straighter in his seat. "I'm glad you think so, sir."

Nordwall opened his arms wide, as if inviting Jimmy into a new world.

"Jimmy, you've been to college. That's a great achievement. But more than that..." Nordwall waited, letting the compliment sink in. "More than that, I truly believe you're one of those rare individuals who really sees how the world works, how business runs, how the market economy makes rich men out of those with the talent."

Jimmy, despite himself, went flush with a mixture of embarrassment and pride. No one in quite a while had picked up on that place within him that set him apart as someone special, someone meant for bigger things. And so Jimmy began listening, his whole being attuned to the vibrations of praise that hung in the air, vibrations that meant something big and good was on its way, like a train barreling down the track. You could feel the air shake, and you knew that train ran a track that led to a destination it was meant for.

Destiny, Jimmy half thought, the feeling if not the word breaking through to his consciousness. *I'm finally coming into what I was meant for.*

"That's about it," Mr. Nordwall was saying. "There'd be a nice little pay increase for you, of course." He stopped and let that sink in before saying, "So, Jimmy, can I count on you? Will you be part of the team that makes this place work?"

Jimmy went home after work with a bounce in his step, dying to tell Mildred the good news.

* * *

Claude Nordwall had spoken with his father for quite some time the night before. As usual, his father had done most of the talking.

"Now, tell me again, son, what you did to run Fred Gratzke off." Fred Gratzke had been handpicked by old Mr. Nordwall to be supervisor down in the Ellijay plant.

"Pop, I didn't do anything," he replied, wishing for the millionth time that he didn't have to explain things five times over every time he talked to his father. "He said, and I quote, 'I'm not living down here with a bunch of hillbillies.' He just didn't like it here, Pop."

"And you're sure you didn't do anything to make him leave?" the old man asked again.

Nordwall waited a few seconds then blew all the air out of his lungs—he couldn't breathe right when he talked business with his dad. "He just said he didn't like it, Pop. Said he didn't know it'd be so different. You know him. He's religious, and there's not a Catholic church anywhere near here."

"Well, son, what do you think needs to be done?" It wasn't just a question—an accusation lingered in the air.

"Replace him." The son gave the short and obvious answer.

"Okay." The old man responded with the even shorter and even more obvious answer.

We'll never get anywhere this way, the son thought.

"Think, son, think. What is it you need?"

"Well, someone to work with the people, talk with

them. Someone loyal to me, but they should like him."

"You need yourself a mule, boy."

"A mule?" Then he wished he hadn't asked it. The exasperated sigh on the other end of the line made his father's message clear: Why do you have to be so stupid?

"You're your mother's son!" the old man finally exclaimed, being in the habit of crediting his son's lack of insight to his wife's side of the family.

"You need someone to do the hard work for you," he continued. "Someone to bear the brunt of labor and take care of unpleasantness you don't have time to deal with," the old man went on, a conciliatory tone seeping into his voice now. "Now Claude, you and I know that you have a grasp on the carpet business like few people do."

"Yes sir, I do know the business," the son replied a bit too quickly, too eagerly lapping up the approval. Claude Nordwall disgusted himself sometimes, but he couldn't help it.

"But you need someone to be the front man, to take the heat. Someone to do the hard work of pulling for you. A mule, boy, and the rest of those plant workers, they're the plow." He waited a second, letting it all sink in with his son.

"You can use a whip, you can use a carrot. Just make sure that mule wants to move and that he'll pull the weight he needs to pull. But you're the boss, remember. You drive that mule. You tell him where he needs to go. Understand, son?"

"So, I need someone local, someone people will

want to work for?" the son asked, beginning to get the point.

"That's right. See if there isn't someone that stands out from the crowd. Someone the people look up to, someone they won't want to cross."

Nordwall thought for a moment. "I think I know someone like that, Pop."

"Yeah? What's he like?"

"He's head of shipping right now. He's had a couple of years of college, which makes him smarter than about anyone else in the plant."

"That could be good," the old man said. "I bet people down there respect a little bit of education."

"Local hero of sorts, too, some years ago," the younger Nordwall continued. "Big football star, played college. Popular, seems. People like him. Clean-cut and good-looking young man."

"Sounds like a mule to me."

"Yes sir, he could well be," Nordwall said, beaming with pride. He knew he'd thought of just the right person.

"Give him a little more money, enough that he likes the taste of it," the old man advised. "Get him used to thinking that he's on your team, like you and he are the ones running things. Between the pride and the money, I bet he'll do about whatever you need him to do."

"Yes sir, I think so, too."

"Well, take it and run with it, son," the old man said. "I'm counting on you, you know."

Claude Nordwall hung up the phone satisfied. He'd talked to his pop, man to man, and gotten the little situation under control. Though things had started off a bit rough, he knew they had worked the problem out.

He laughed to himself. A mule. He'd thought of the perfect mule. This would be a nice story to go home and tell his wife—how he and his pop had worked through a personnel problem, and how his pop had jumped at his suggestion of who to hire for plant supervisor.

And a day later, he had another good story for his wife—how Jimmy Jackson had jumped at the opportunity to work as Claude Nordwall's mule.

"Things will be looking up," Jimmy told Mildred. "More money. More respect. And it all starts now, today."

Mildred gave Jimmy a big kiss. "Well, then, after the young'uns go to sleep, we'll just have to have a little celebration, won't we?"

Jimmy replied with relish, "Like I said, the start of good things!"

Mildred took on a serious air. "Jimmy, I'm really proud of you."

She meant it, and he knew it. To tell the truth, he was pretty proud of himself.

Chapter 6

"I knew there was something up after Wagon Train Day," Mildred said, holding her cup out for another refill. "Decaf, right?" she asked.

"One hundred percent unleaded," Caleb replied. "You'll sleep like a baby."

"Naw, I don't go to bed 'til late anymore anyway," Mildred replied. "Besides, I hold coffee like some men hold liquor. Take more than what you got to put me under—or get me up, anyway."

"What about Wagon Train?" Joyce asked.

"That's when I first noticed something seemed wrong with Jim. All of a sudden, nothing much suited him anymore, except for what wasn't connected with Smoky Hollow or Ellijay or anyplace where, as he used to say, 'The action ain't.' I asked him once what action he was going on about, and he didn't have much of an answer.

"Looking back, I think it wasn't so much a matter of wanting something as it was *not* wanting something.

Jim just didn't want to be who he was. And I sure didn't like who he was trying to be. I just didn't realize it until that Wagon Train Day."

Mildred patted Fancy on the neck and pulled a sugar cube out of her pocket. "Hey, here's a treat for a pretty girl." She had just saddled her up, and she stood there feeling the mare's soft lips on her palm and thinking about how much she enjoyed having her. When she was little, her mamma had let her take a pony ride when a small-time carnival had come through Ellijay. From that day on, she had begged for a horse of her own.

"Now where you reckon we'll put a horse?" her mamma had asked her. "Make a bedroom for it? We're not set up for a horse, Mildred." Her mamma had looked down at her disappointed face and softened.

"Maybe when you're a little older, we can ask Mr. Bridges to let you ride his horses now and again." She thought a minute. "He might be up for that. I know some other young'uns he used to let ride—showed 'em how and all."

Little Mildred beamed. "And then I can get my own someday!" she exclaimed.

"Well," her mamma told her, "that someday'll have to be when you can do for yourself, 'cause I ain't no horse person, and neither is your daddy."

"But when I get big enough, I can have my own horse?" Mildred asked.

"Honey, when you're old enough, you can have any-thing you can figure out how to get."

Mildred thought back to that conversation every now and then, especially when she was brushing down Fancy.

She'd saved a little money while she was teaching and still living at home—didn't hardly have much in the way of expenses. So once she and Jimmy got married, she'd thought herself old enough, just like her mamma had said. The roan quarter horse had arrived at their home well before little Johnny had.

"Look at Mamma's big horsie!" three-year-old Johnny screamed now, running toward Mildred. As she led Fancy out of the barn, she swooped her little three-year-old ball of energy into the air and gave him a big kiss.

"Are you excited about Wagon Train?" she asked him.

"Yeah!" the little boy said enthusiastically, not really knowing what Wagon Train was all about but roused up just because it sounded like something grand.

"You gonna wave at Mamma when she rides by on Fancy?" Mildred asked.

Little Johnny just started waving his arm like mad in reply. By now Jimmy had come up, Rachel lying comfortably in the crook of his arm.

"Well," Jimmy said, "we're gonna run on out to the Logans' and set up. You be sure and ride careful."

"Oh, I will," Mildred replied. "You keep a good eye on this one," she added as she nuzzled Johnny, who squealed with delight. "After we ride by, you can take Rachel on to Mamma's, and I'll meet up with you and Johnny on the square."

"Sounds good to me," Jimmy replied. "See you there." A hurried peck served as a goodbye kiss, Jimmy took Johnny, and they headed off for the car.

Mildred loved Wagon Train Day. Every year in July,

the Gilmer County and Murray County Saddle Clubs got together with horses and wagons (some covered, some not) for a trek over the mountain from Chatsworth to Ellijay, followed by a big celebration in town. It was like a history celebration, a trail ride, a parade, and carnival rolled into one—one of the best days of the year.

Some folks from Ellijay would ride over the day before, going into Chatsworth for the night, just about twenty miles away. Others, like Mildred, would just meet up with the clubs somewhere along the way. Since Smoky Hollow lay just off Chatsworth Highway, the road between Chatsworth and Ellijay, she'd planned to join the group as they came by.

"Ready for a nice ride, Fancy?" Mildred asked. The mare stomped the ground and shook her head as if to say, "Let's get going." So Mildred swung into the saddle and started off down the road toward the highway.

She'd timed it just right. The first of the horses came around a bend in the road just as she made it to the highway. Jimmy had cut it close—fifteen minutes later and he might have been stuck. Once the wagon train came by, there was no getting around it.

Fancy snorted and pranced a bit at the sight of the group. Mildred circled her, walked her up the road a ways, then came back, waving at several familiar faces as she and Fancy melted into the crowd.

The day was perfect for a ride—eighty degrees and not too humid. The clouds were a welcome presence— nothing about them said rain, and they spotted the sky in just the right quantity. Mildred and Fancy moved along partly in warm sunshine, partly in a nice shade. Mildred relaxed into that wonderful sense of being one with her horse, keeping the same rhythm, marking time by the monotonous clacking of hooves.

The Logan place stood just outside of town. As she rode by, Mildred saw Logans and Withrows and Holts all mingled together, a lawn-chair metropolis alongside the road, with her husband and the children right in the middle. The riders waved to the people along the parade route. People waved back.

Jimmy was nursing a tall glass of lemonade, which he raised to her in salute as she rode by. Little Johnny hollered and carried on like he was seeing the greatest spectacle of his short life. Then he saw his mamma.

Jimmy had never lost the limp from his foot accident, but he still had enough of his football reflexes and speed to jump out of his chair and grab the little boy as he took off for the road. Didn't even spill a drop of lemonade, Mildred noticed with admiration. Little Johnny let out a delighted squeal as his daddy swooped him up and carried him back to the chairs.

As the wagon train wound around its route through town, Mildred broke off and headed east. Most of the riders would head south down to the fairgrounds and to the saddle-club rink. But Mildred's sister Liz's place was just a fifteen-minute walk from town. Liz's husband kept a few head of cattle, so their property sported a barn and a fenced-in pasture. Mildred would leave Fancy there and walk into town to meet up with Jimmy and Johnny, stopping at her mamma's along the way.

Mildred dismounted, opened the pasture gate, and led Fancy in. A hitching post stood right outside the barn. Mildred pulled off the bit and bridle, took the lead rope from the halter, and wrapped it around the post.

She patted Fancy's rump as she made her way around to the barn. That was the first lesson Mr. Bridges had taught her—if you're out of the horse's line of vision, always let it know by touch where you stand. "Keep more of your teeth that way," he had told her with a gummy grin.

After squaring away the tack, Mildred talked to Fancy while she rubbed her down good, wiping away the sweat from an honest morning's walk. "Such a pretty horse," she said as she pulled the dandy brush across the rippling body, "all fourteen hands of you." When she thought she had done a passable job, Mildred finished up with the hoof pick. Then she unwrapped the lead rope from the hitching post and removed Fancy's halter. "Have yourself a nice rest of the day, beautiful," she said, giving the horse an affectionate pat on the neck.

Within the hour, Mildred stood on the front porch of her mamma's house. She had walked over to take a quick bath and grab a change of clothes—though she loved the smell of horses, she knew it didn't wear well as perfume. Now, refreshed and ready to head for the town square, she leaned on the porch rail. Her mother, Lois, swung gently back and forth on the porch swing, enjoying the gift of a fine July day that wasn't too hot. Her daddy sat in a rocker, little Rachel on his knee. Her uncle Robert, who lived with her parents, had already walked to town to watch the wagon train.

Then, just as she thought about moseying on to town herself, her mamma started talking. And as the story unfolded, it seemed to take the beauty out of the summer day.

"All I'm telling you is what I heard. Bill Craig said

that Jimmy talked awful rough with some of the folks t'other day. Said he accused them of not working hard enough."

"Well, mamma, Jimmy is the supervisor," Mildred put in. "That means that sometimes he's gonna rub people the wrong way."

She said it without much conviction. Just from what Jimmy said at home, she thought he seemed kinda hard on the folks down at the mill. Still, she wanted to give him the benefit of the doubt. He was working long hours these days and coming home grouchy, and she figured he just needed to let off some steam.

"Honey," Lois said, "I've known Bill Craig all my borned days. He ain't perfect by any means, but I can't say that I've ever heard anybody say he's lazy.

"Here's the point of me telling you this," she went on. "Just so you can be prepared. I let that husband of yours know what I thought about him comin' down on Bill. And he didn't like it much." Lois paused a second. "So when y'all come to get Rachel, you shouldn't expect him to want to hang around."

Great, Mildred thought. She knew her mamma well enough to know she'd done a little bit more than just let Jimmy know what she thought. She'd probably given him a considerable piece of her mind. And no one wanted to hang around after getting one of Lois Holt's tongue-lashings.

Mildred sighed. Jimmy had been hard enough to live with lately. "So, what'd you say to him, Mamma?"

"Just what I told you," Lois said. "Bill Craig don't ever laze about. If he told Jimmy he was working as hard and fast as he could, then you could bet a coon's skin he was."

"What else, Mamma?" Mildred asked the question with a tone of resignation in her voice.

"Not much really," Lois said. Then she peered over her glasses at Mildred and fixed her with one of the looks that stopped most folks midsentence when Lois gave it. "He just said he reckoned him and me had a little disagreement about things. I told him weren't no disagreement; he was just plain wrong."

Mildred imagined how that would have gone down, given the mood of her husband lately.

"Then he says to me, 'With all due respect…'" A withering tone made Lois's voice a blunt weapon, ready to beat to death anyone without the sense to get out of earshot.

Mildred's shoulders slumped. She could see this was going nowhere good in a hurry.

"And?"

"And nothing," Lois said. "Just cut him off right then and there and said, 'Sonny, I ain't never heard nothing but foolishness follow them words you just spoke.'" Lois sat silent for a minute and let what she'd said sink in. Then she went on, "And I ain't. Jimmy left right then, not much to say."

"Oh, Mamma," was all Mildred could think to reply.

Chapter 7

Mildred hurried into town, looking for Jimmy. She started out at the dunking tank, which Jimmy loved. Throwing balls there reminded him that he'd once thrown a football with a fair amount of accuracy. But she saw no sign of Jimmy.

She wandered on around the square. She looked inside the drugstore, thinking maybe Jimmy and Johnny had stopped to get something at the fountain, though there were plenty of people hawking food outside. No such luck. Finally, she saw Jimmy standing over where the watermelon-spitting contest would be. Next to that, there had been a pie contest that a rich, golden-crusted pecan pie had won. Jimmy held little Johnny's hand on one side. His boss, Mr. Nordwall, was on the other.

Mildred sidled up to Johnny and Jimmy. "Hey, y'all."

Johnny squealed. "Mamma!" he yelled. "I saw you on Fancy!"

"Yes, you did," Mildred answered. "Did you have fun watching all the horses and wagons?"

Johnny replied by throwing his head back and doing his best horse neigh imitation, which was mostly like hollering. But Mildred got the point. Johnny had liked seeing all the horses.

"Johnny!" Jimmy exclaimed, giving the boy's arm a tug. "Don't yell right in our ears. Me and Mr. Nordwall are trying to talk."

"Aw, Jimmy, he's just letting off a little steam," Mildred said, thinking Jimmy a little rough on their son.

Jimmy turned toward his wife and, without as much as a howdy-do, said, "I'm trying to talk here. Can't do that with so much yelling going on."

Jimmy then turned back to his conversation with Mr. Nordwall. To Mildred, they didn't seem to be talking about anything too important.

If Jimmy had bothered to look at his wife, he might have had the sense to see the storm coming. Mildred was a patient woman, especially compared to her mamma. But now a scowl formed on her brow like a thundertop in July. She didn't like the way Jimmy had been acting lately or the idea of him mistreating people at the plant. And she especially didn't like being treated like she was wasting her husband's precious time. She'd walked up to town worried about how Jimmy'd be feeling after his run-in with her mamma. But he didn't seem to be concerned about her feelings one little bit.

That's why Mildred said what she did, which was the one thing that would most embarrass her husband.

"Jimmy," she said in a voice her husband could not ignore and that Mr. Nordwall could very plainly hear.

"Aren't you planning on getting in on the watermelon-seed-spitting contest?" Her instincts told her that, more than anything else, Jimmy didn't want to appear to Mr. Nordwall as somebody who'd spit seeds.

Mr. Nordwall snorted a laugh. Jimmy wheeled around on his wife, his attention full on her now. She could practically see the cogs and wheels spinning in his head. All at the same time, he was trying to figure out how to apologize to Mildred without it sounding like an apology to Mr. Nordwall, how to get her to not be mad and drop whatever it was she was doing, how to sound manly and in charge to Mr. Nordwall, and how to change the subject to something else and start moving away before all the spitting started. Which meant, of course, that what managed to make its way out was about the lamest thing he could have said.

"Aw, honey, no need to joke in front of Mr. Nordwall." His eyes pleaded with hers. "Why don't we go get some food? Hungry, Mr. Nordwall?"

"Hot dogs! Hot dogs!" Johnny started yelling. Jimmy didn't act as if he needed to settle his son down now.

"Well, if you're good and hungry, we'll get us some hot dogs," Jimmy said as he scooped up the little boy.

"But I could sure use the five dollars in prize money," Mildred said, standing where Jimmy couldn't run off. "Why, Mr. Nordwall," Mildred went on, "Not only did Jimmy enter the contest last year; he won!" Her fake giddiness was such that even Mr. Nordwall caught on that something was up.

"Perhaps we should go on and eat, Mrs. Jackson. That is, unless, you're going to enter the competition yourself."

"No thank you, sir," Mildred said, realizing that Mr. Nordwall was setting himself up on Jimmy's side, trying to embarrass her. "Takes somebody with a lot more practice at spitting than me."

"Indeed," Mr. Nordwall replied. The way he said it, Mildred thought he implied that she could hit a spittoon from ten yards out.

Mildred knew now that unless she wanted to take apart Jimmy's boss in a public place, she'd better retreat. She wasn't foolish enough to think that Jimmy didn't need his job. "I'll take Johnny on back to Mamma's to eat," she said, taking the boy from Jimmy and putting back on some semblance of a sunny look. "I'm kind of tuckered out from riding today." That really wasn't true, but once Mildred decided to retreat, she was as good as gone. She'd regroup once she got home. Looking at Jimmy with a sweetness that he knew covered hurt feelings, she said, "You stay and enjoy yourself. I'll get Mamma to take us home after we've had a bite."

Jimmy just looked at her. He knew better than to try and suggest otherwise.

Mildred turned to trek back to her mamma's. Just then, over a megaphone, a man behind the pie contest table announced, "Now that the judging is over, let the eating commence. Pecan pie for sale by the slice. Come and get your fill."

Mildred's face burned red with anger as she walked away. Mr. Nordwall's words rang in her ears all the way back to her mamma's place. "Pee-can pie," Mr. Nordwall said, emphasizing the way the man had said it, with a long *e*. "Makes it sound like a urinal, doesn't it, Jackson? Pee-can pie." Nordwall laughed. Then he asked, "Why can't people speak properly around here?"

Mildred's face grew redder as she walked, realizing that the last words she'd heard were Jimmy's: "Just a bunch of hillbillies who don't know how to talk right."

Mildred sat out on her back porch. She loved being outside after the children had been tucked into bed. Nice quiet time, it was. She sat and tried to sort out what in the world had happened. Now that she was home, being a sensible woman, she knew that besides being mad she ought to be worried.

She looked out over her backyard. She'd spent a lot of time out there. Everybody knew she had a green thumb, and she could get just about anything to come up. She loved to just sit and look at the trees and plants and flowers she had grown.

Her eyes came to rest on a rosebush next to the back steps. She loved that bush, whose clusters of small, pale-pink flowers gave off a peppery aroma. It could be traced back to the rosebush her granny had tied up behind her house, off of her back porch. Once her granny died, her mamma made some cuttings and rooted them at her house, and Mildred had done the same off one of her mamma's plants. Something peaceful overtook her every time she'd let her mind relax and just take in that rosebush—the way it looked, the way it smelled, what it said about who she was and where she came from and what was important.

By the time Jimmy got home and came outside, Mildred had made up her mind that fighting with him was the wrong way to go. More than anything else, what she had seen in town made her sad—her husband so eager for his boss's approval that he'd say anything to get on Nordwall's good side. Or, maybe that was too harsh. But it came close enough to worry Mildred.

She knew he came with a peace offering. She was glad to see he at least retained the good sense for that. "Hey, sweetheart," he said as he handed her a cold Coke and a bowl of lime sherbet—her favorite summertime treat.

She took the peace offering and made one of her own. "I love it out here," she said. "I love you out here."

She meant to remind Jimmy of a night in the late spring, not too long ago. The moon had hung full in the sky, so full that the weight of it seemed to pull it down to earth. The children had long since been put to bed for the night. With the scent of honeysuckle heavy in the air, she and Jimmy had spent a romantic time outside, a blanket covering the hard wood and splinters of the picnic table. She had pulled the slender stem from the middle of several of the honeysuckle flowers, nectar dripping from the ends, and touched them to his tongue. The night had glowed with the embers of gentleness. It was the best time she could remember, at least recently.

But Jimmy didn't remember, or at least he didn't take the hint. "I don't know," he said. "Do you really like it here, Mildred, out in the middle of nowhere?"

Mildred slowly swirled her lime sherbet. "Don't you?" she asked, turning the question around, feeling for where Jimmy was headed.

"Well," he said, "for starters, there's nobody out

here. Don't you ever get lonesome, just you and the young'uns?"

"Not just me and the young'uns," Mildred replied. "Me and the young'uns and you."

"You know what I mean." Jimmy took on an exasperated tone.

"No, I don't," Mildred replied. "If I need to see anybody, that's no trouble. Johnny and Rachel have a nice place to play, and there's a barn for Fancy. I like my yard and garden. We have a nice house, Jimmy. I grew up back in here, at least I practically did when Granny was alive. Gone to church out here about all my life. We've got people who'd do about anything for us, if we ask, and we're close enough to help out if your mamma and the boys need it." And she knew they did need it— Jimmy still helped out around his mamma's place quite a bit. There were some things that Billy and Harold just weren't very good at.

Mildred stopped for a minute and did what she always did. About halfway through her sherbet, she'd pour about a good third of her Coke into the bowl and make herself a sherbet float. After sipping a little from the bowl, tasting the lime-flavored Coke, she looked back at Jimmy. He slouched in his lawn chair. From the outside light she could see well enough that his hair stood straight up, like he had been pulling at it. And she knew that, in a better light, she'd see the worry lines that had started to form on his face.

"What is it, Jimmy?" she asked.

He let out a long, tired sigh. "It's not easy, being the boss," Jimmy said. "I like those people, too. Not just you, and not just your mamma. Lots of them are my friends. I even got Harold working there now."

"I know that, Jimmy." He had found a spot for his brother shortly after his promotion, knowing the extra money from the mill would help his mother.

"Thing is, I gotta learn how to be boss," Jimmy went on. "And that means not everybody's gonna like me."

"I know that, too," Mildred said.

"I should've been nicer today," Jimmy said. "And Mr. Nordwall, he's not so good with people. So maybe he shouldn't have been teasing you, either."

Mildred listened. She knew more was coming.

"Still, he's our ticket out, sweetheart," he said. "I know you don't seem to want it, but I bet you'd like living somewhere bigger, somewhere better. You liked it down in Athens, didn't you, when you and me went to school?"

Mildred nodded. Athens had been nice enough, though she figured she mainly liked the fact that it was different. She knew it'd wear off in the long run.

"What about Dalton?" Jimmy went on. "Not far from here, but a bigger town. Not everyone knows your business. I could work in a place where I didn't have to worry about hurting people's feelings because they wouldn't be friends, just workers."

Of everything Mildred heard that night, and every time she thought back to that particular Wagon Train night, it was those words she remembered; remembered how they should have been a warning, big red flashers: *They wouldn't be friends. Just workers.*

"What are we talking about, Jimmy?" Mildred asked. "Really?"

With a measure each of pride, caution, and stubbornness, Jimmy said, "Mr. Nordwall thinks his daddy's gonna open another carpet plant in a couple of years." He rushed on before Mildred could get out a "so what."

"Now, Mr. Nordwall says he likes running the Ellijay mill just fine. Says his other brother has all he can do just to keep up at the other two mills in Dalton." Jimmy hurried on, excitement fanning his voice now.

"Mr. Nordwall says that if I do a real good job, showing I can run a plant as supervisor, it'd mean I'd be putting myself in good stead with the family, as one who can be counted on. He said…" Jimmy's voice now dropped almost to a barely contained whisper, like he was letting out a secret that nobody should know about yet but was so good it had to be spoken.

"He said," Jimmy repeated, "that his daddy'd look favorably on me as being the one to run the new plant." He beamed as he let the words sink in, caution thrown to the wind. Now that he'd heard them out of his own mouth, he knew them to be so sensible, so full of good things, conveyors of a future brighter than they could have hoped for, that Mildred couldn't possibly tsk-tsk him on this thing.

"Jimmy," Mildred said, weighing her words carefully, "I'd follow you wherever your heart takes you." Jimmy flashed a broad grin. He reached over to take Mildred's hand, and she let him. Then she squeezed really hard.

"But honey," she said, and at the sound of those two words Jimmy's grin fell hard. "But honey, what if it doesn't work out that way? Have you thought of that?"

Jimmy pulled his hand back. "What's the matter with you, Mildred? Can't you even listen for a minute to some good news? Can't you figure out that not everybody is all head over heels about backwoods Smoky Hollow?"

Jimmy's voice grew husky. "I've lived here all my life, you know, and I've never seen what's so great about being nobody from nowhere. A bunch of poorer-than-dirt hicks who can't do nothin' but work for other men. Only thing people here are famous for is running 'shine. That's just great." He stood up and walked over to the door. "No thanks," he said. "That's not my life." And as he went in he said, "And it's not yours, and it's not our Johnny's and Rachel's. Quit thinking about just yourself and think about them."

And so Mildred did, long after the fizz had died away in her sherbet float.

"Anyway," Mildred said, "we had some rough months of it after Wagon Train. Not fighting, exactly, but not really at peace, either. Seemed we were both always walking on eggshells, you know, and that didn't much suit me."

"No!" Caleb said, eyes wide with mock surprise.

"You old smarty pants," Mildred said, slapping Caleb's arm and shaking her head at Joyce. "How do you put up with him?"

Joyce laughed. "We all have our burdens."

Chapter 8

The year moved on, though not fast enough to suit Mildred. The days seemed to drag, and life took on a kind of "gotta do it" drudgery, though she still did what she could to make home seem homey. If little Johnny had been something other than a little boy mostly ready for rambunctiousness, he might have noticed the sadness that hung around his mamma's smile. Or maybe not. No one else noticed, either. Most of the time, Mildred herself didn't even know it was happening.

It would have been easier, in a way, to be smoldering mad at Jimmy and have him be mad at her. An out-and-out battle would almost have been a relief. Instead, they lived in a kind of polite truce, without arguments but without much feeling between them either. Little things slipped away.

She stood looking out her kitchen door one day through the frosty morning pane. It hadn't been a heavy frost, just enough to make the grass shine. The sun hit the grass and made it sparkle, but not for long. The sun's touch gently wiped away the ice.

Then something caught Mildred's eye. She noticed that, where the shadow of a tree fell, the frost remained. Jimmy walked into the kitchen about then; he had to grab the dinner pail Mildred had made up for him. And as Jimmy strolled through, a little voice said inside her head as her eyes swept over the view, an island of frost in a sea of sunshine.

Mildred had always had an eye for the beauties of nature, and she had a touch of the poet about her. She could put words to the feelings she had when she looked at the world.

The first time she did that when they were together, Jimmy had stood in awe of her. Driving down the road after a brief summer shower, they'd seen a rainbow. "Hey, look at that," Jimmy had said, being the first to spot it. "A rainbow. Just a part, not a whole thing, all straight like that."

"That's not a rainbow," Mildred said. "It's a rainstick."

"A rainstick?" Jimmy asked.

"Well, it's not really bowed. It's straight, like a stick. So it's a rainstick."

Jimmy laughed.

"Hey, and look over there," Mildred said, "another one."

"Where?"

"On the other side of the sun." Looking toward the horizon on either side of the sun lay two straight-line rainbows.

"Have you ever seen such?" Jimmy asked.

"Kaleidoscope roads to heaven," Mildred said.

"What's that mean?"

"Haven't you ever used a kaleidoscope?" Mildred asked. "You know, they're like tubes with an eyehole. You look in one end, and there's all sorts of mixed up colors you see from the light coming in."

"Yeah." Jimmy thought for a minute. "Hey, that makes sense."

"Well, of course it does," she replied, laughing.

"I don't know how you think of these things," he said, reaching over to hold her hand. By the way he squeezed, Mildred could feel that Jimmy thought she was wonderful.

After that, it had become a given, one of the assumptions in a marriage that serves as a foundation stone. Mildred would see the world and come up with ways to talk about it that made the looking seem brand-new, and Jimmy would always squeeze her hand in appreciation for the good things she helped him see.

And that was what was so bad about that frosty autumn morning.

Mildred looked out, saw something brimming over with a type of beauty, thought about how to say it, and then let it pass. A barely audible sigh escaped her lips as Jimmy walked over, kissed her head, and told her, "I'll probably be late coming home again tonight."

"Should I hold supper?" Mildred asked.

"Naw," Jimmy said. "You and the young'uns go ahead and eat. Don't want you waiting on me."

And with that little bit of practiced politeness, Jimmy went to work. Those days, Mildred and the children ate supper without him more and more. Part of her wished he would ask her to wait, to eat with him. But he didn't, and she didn't feel like doing it without him asking. So she ate without him, and the wall between them grew a little taller every day.

On this particular morning, Mildred busied herself with the house and the children. At one point, she found herself staring at little Rachel, and tears formed in her eyes because she was thinking how Jimmy was with his little children. She knew some husbands didn't count for two cents when it came to how they took up with their children. But Jimmy held Rachel like she was the most precious thing in the world. And Mildred cried for just a minute, thinking about how obvious it was that Jimmy loved his little daughter and that he would do anything to protect her. And though he roughhoused with Johnny, he never got too rough. And Mildred had seen him touch his son's face as he slept, a caress that lingered and spoke love through the fingers.

He's a good man, she thought. And that made the sadness worse.

By the afternoon, Mildred had done everything that needed doing around the house. Rachel and Johnny both lay napping; Mildred knew that she wouldn't be able to count on these little afternoon breaks much longer because Johnny already showed signs of not wanting— or needing—a nap. But today, with both of the kids snoozing away, she had a little time to herself.

She would have given anything back in August for a free afternoon. She had canned the whole month away, it seemed, putting up for winter. By the time corn, beans, tomatoes, and okra had been put up, she sometimes felt as if she were made of nothing but steam, all that hot boiling water on hot boiling August days. But now it was fall, and she had the time, but she didn't quite know what she wanted to do.

She picked up a book. Mildred loved to read, so Jimmy had subscribed to the People's Book Club that Sears ran. The first book they got, by Shirley Seifert, had been about Jefferson Davis and his wife, Varina. A blurb inside proudly proclaimed that Mrs. Seifert lived in St. Louis, Missouri, and had been nominated for the Pulitzer writing prize.

Mildred had liked Mrs. Seifert's book, but she just couldn't seem to get into the second book from Sears, by a man named Victor Canning. It was called *The Golden Salamander,* but it didn't seem all that golden to Mildred. It just never caught her fancy, despite the fact that it was supposed to be exciting and had even been made into a movie. She had never seen it. She knew by now that the Sears club picked up books that had been out a while. The movie had come out in 1950. Jimmy was right; the best and newest of everything didn't make it to Smoky Hollow right away.

She put down her book and ambled over to the phonograph—another of Jimmy's purchases, bought on time like everything he ordered now. Jimmy had paid five dollars down; he seemed to think the balance of one hundred ninety-three dollars wouldn't be too hard to pay—ten dollars a month is what it came out to.

Mildred's mamma had warned her about such when Mildred had started out teaching, and she carried her mother's penchant for paying cash when possible, doing without when she couldn't. But here stood the new Silvertone, and Mildred had to admit she enjoyed having it.

She remembered how excited Jimmy had been as he read from the catalog: "Best Silvertone hi-fi console phono-graph…two-section cabinet…three matched speakers…. Amplifier has twenty-watt output." He'd turned down page 837 of the catalog for easy reference so they could look at it and anticipate its arrival.

Shortly after the phonograph came, Jimmy had decid-ed to get records from Sears as well. They had what they called the Silvertone Record Club. Between the book club and the record club, Mildred figured Sears kept people pretty entertained. And Jimmy had been eyeing a new television set in the Sears catalog as well—a bigger and better one than they already had.

Mildred decided to pass over the couple of vinyl plat-ters that had come as an introduction to the record club. Neither Pat Boone nor Lawrence Welk appealed to her at the moment. Instead, she flipped through the handful of records that she especially loved, mostly gospel.

She almost put on the Blackwood Brothers' *Hymn Sing.* She especially enjoyed listening to J. D. Sumner, who wasn't a Blackwood brother by blood but still sang with them. He could go so low his voice practically fell off the very end of the piano. Finally, though, she opted for the LeFevres.

Two years earlier, Mildred and Jimmy had gone down to visit her aunt Doris in Canton, and her uncle Robert had come along for the ride. He wanted to see his sister Doris, of course. But he was like Mildred, a singer, and part of his reason for going was a Saturday night gospel sing in Canton at the high school auditorium. The LeFevres were there, and the audience practically stormed the stage that night. There had been clapping and stomping and singing. Those folks knew how to put on a show.

So it was the LeFevres that Mildred listened to for a short while that afternoon. Of course, Mildred especially liked Eva Mae, the only woman in the group. Sometimes Mildred wondered what it would be like to travel around like Eva Mae did, singing and making records. The thought crossed Mildred's mind that she sang pretty well, and that maybe she and Uncle Robert ought to do more than just perform around the county. Maybe they could even get a few more folks to join them—more voices, more instruments. She and Uncle Robert always sang just with him playing the guitar. But maybe they could do more.

But then Mildred realized it wasn't more she wanted—just different. Something different from what was eating up her days. And as Mildred sat on the couch, trying to figure her way past an obstacle there didn't seem to be any rhyme or reason to, she heard Eva Mae singing through the new Silvertone. As the words "He washed my eyes with tears" filled the room, tears once again filled Mildred's eyes. And for a time that lasted as long as the children's nap, her feelings ran like two little creeks down her face.

When a feud smolders but the parties are bent on making things nice, it doesn't look like a feud to anyone else. Routines persisted, as did the Friday night rook games. Mildred and Jimmy had always loved to throw cards. Even better, they liked to play against each other. Boys against girls—that's the way they always did it.

"Gonna shoot the moon for sure this time," Alice

declared as she dealt out the hand. She threw a green fourteen up as the last card on top of the kitty.

Despite it all, Mildred enjoyed these Friday night games. She and Alice had been friends a long time, and Jimmy and Tony had hit it off when they were introduced to each other back when Jimmy was courting Mildred. Tony had a sizable apple orchard that he had gotten from his daddy, and he grew apples full time. He had helped Mildred and Jimmy start their own small orchard.

Tony and Alice had a little boy about Johnny's age, and they brought him along on rook nights. The two played hard together. But with three-year-olds there comes a time when it's like an "off" switch has been thrown, so that one minute the two little boys would be running headlong into everything in the house, and the next minute they'd be fast asleep. That always signaled the start of the rook game.

Mildred sat at the table now, nursing her sweet tea. Her blue moods came and went, but tonight things seemed pretty much on an even keel. It didn't hurt that she had had the rook twice in a row already.

Mildred smiled. She silently counted down her hand—the thirteen, twelve, ten, eight, and seven of green. The rook card sat in the middle of it all, casting her a sideways glance that signaled a conspiracy of sorts. Jimmy and Tony would yell "cheat" for sure, two of the three rooks coming off her and Alice's deals. Of course, the protest was good-natured. Both men knew that neither of the women could stack a deck if their lives depended on it and that they wouldn't if they could. The two women got an incredible amount of pleasure out of beating their husbands the old-fashioned way—fair and square. With the green fourteen, Mildred knew they'd be out this time. Three hands to get to three hundred points. That would warm the heart of any rook player.

The bidding started. Mildred cut through all the nonsense and said: "A hundred." But before Jimmy had a chance to counter, the telephone rang.

"I'll get it," Jimmy said. Mildred took another sip of her tea, savoring the knowledge of a hand already won. Jimmy would never have been so eager to answer the phone if he had a hand worth anything at all.

Jimmy came back shortly, and Mildred knew right away that something bad had happened. Jimmy had gone all pale, and he shook his head as if to throw out the words he'd just heard, shake them out of his ears.

"What's wrong, Jimmy?" Mildred asked, afraid he might tell her something she didn't want to hear.

Jimmy placed his hands on the back of the kitchen chair. He shook his head again, and his voice tumbled out cracked as a dropped egg. "Bill Craig's dead. Hit by a train."

Everybody's jaw dropped at the same time.

Finally, Mildred asked, "Do you know how it happened?"

"No," Jimmy said. "Mrs. Craig wants to talk to you, not me."

Mildred jumped up and went to the phone. Jimmy just stood there, staring at the table. He started to shake. He asked, loud enough for Alice and Tony to hear, soft enough for them to know that they shouldn't answer, "Why would this suit me? I ain't never had nothing against Bill." Alice and Tony knew the question hadn't been asked of them, so they kept respectfully silent.

Mildred walked back in. "My gosh. Hit by a train."

Again silence filled the room as each one contemplated being hit by a train. They had all seen Andy Seller's car after it was smashed a few years back.

"Mrs. Craig wants me and Uncle Robert to sing at the funeral," Mildred said at last.

That seemed to bring a sense of normality back to the table. Of course, Mildred and Robert would sing, just like they sang at most funerals up around Smoky Hollow. And after an obligatory time of getting the awfulness out of their systems by talking about it, Tony and Alice gathered up their little boy and took off for the night.

"Reckon I'd better let Mr. Nordwall know," Jimmy said, going for the phone. "He'll want to know, Bill being an employee and all."

Mildred thought Mr. Nordwall would want to know a lot less than Jimmy assumed. But she knew it was the right thing to do—to call and tell the plant manager about the tragedy that had just happened to one of his workers.

Chapter 9

All eyes fell on Mildred and Robert as they sang. They had worked up a version of "Near the Cross" because Mrs. Craig had told them at the funeral home that she loved that old song.

Jimmy sat there thinking how nice Mrs. Craig had been to Mildred at the visitation—and how cold she had acted toward him. When Jimmy finally had the chance to speak with her, he'd said, "My sincerest condolences." He had practiced the phrase, trying to give it the weight he felt the big words expressed.

"Reckon that's just a fancy way of saying sorry," Mrs. Craig had replied, fixing her eye on Jimmy. "People orta save their sorries for when they mean it." Then she had turned and walked away, leaving Jimmy with an outstretched hand that had never been taken.

So Jimmy squirmed through much of the service. He couldn't help but feel uncomfortable, especially because of the orders Mr. Nordwall had given him when they last talked.

"Too bad, too bad," Nordwall had said when he heard the news. "A real pity, hit by a train like that."

"Yes sir, it is," Jimmy had said.

"But business is business," Mr. Nordwall went on, "and I just can't get away."

"But the funeral's on Sunday," Jimmy put in.

"Yes, I know," Mr. Nordwall replied, sounding a bit peevish at being reminded. "But the weekend's the only time I can get over to Dalton to talk over some things with my brother." Nordwall waited a minute for a "that's okay, then," but since it wasn't forthcoming, he went on with an impatient sigh. "Carpet business, Jackson, carpet business. Can't be helped."

Shortly after that, Jimmy had discovered Mr. Nordwall was putting him in charge of delivering official mill condolences. That's where he'd first gotten the idea to use the word *condolences,* when Mr. Nordwall said it. But Saturday's visitation hadn't gone very well, and Jimmy hadn't gotten beyond his own personal attestation of how sorry he was about the accident. So now he was left with the unpleasant task of speaking on behalf of the mill. Jimmy didn't like it; but Nordwall had said that as second in charge he had to stand in, like the vice president of the United States would sometimes stand in for the president at overseas funerals. That had made Jimmy feel a little better, because it made his role seem important, though deep inside he knew Nordwall was pushing an unpleasant task off on him.

Thinking about his conversation with Mr. Nordwall and his coming conversation with Mrs. Craig occupied Jimmy's mind so fully for a few minutes that he completely forgot where he was. Finally, though, the sweet harmony of the funeral song struck Jimmy's ears and coaxed him back to the moment. Mildred's voice always seemed to cut through whatever mood he was in and touch his heart. He thought back to his own daddy's funeral and remembered how her singing had made it seem angels were watching over them all. Then he thought the same about his baptism—how he had gone down into the waters of death, then been raised to new life with the notes of Mildred's song still ringing in his ears. He tried to take comfort in that, though the prospect of what he had to do still weighed on his mind.

Mildred and Robert had been switching off, doing alternate solos on the verses, always singing together on the refrain. Now they finished together, singing,

> In the cross, in the cross,
> Be my glory ever;
> Till my raptured soul shall find
> Rest beyond the river.

The church filled with *amens* and tears sparkled in many eyes as Mildred and Robert sat down. Preacher Wingate then took over the service, weighing in with the same life-and-death message he'd preached at Junior Jackson's funeral. There were no soft transitions, no sweet sympathies extended to the family. Instead, he went about doing what he had always heard done—using the funeral as an occasion to warn the listeners of the dangers of hellfire and invite them to accept the cooling fountain of life.

For what seemed like an eternity to Jimmy, Preacher Wingate preached on. Jimmy was so eaten up with bad feelings, he didn't even try to absorb the pulpit-slapping lessons Preacher Wingate laid down that day.

Finally, everybody around Jimmy seemed to be getting up, and so he stood up, too. Jimmy fumbled around, trying to figure out what page number he should turn to. As the pianist beat the old Acrosonic piano with a tempo that signaled victory and assurance over death, the congregation started singing. After thumbing through the pages, Jimmy caught up with the congregation as they sang the last verse:

What have I to dread, what have I to fear,
Leaning on the everlasting arms;
I have blessed peace with my Lord so near,
Leaning on the everlasting arms.

Preacher Wingate threw up his hand. This tactic often served him well. Folks knew to stop singing when that hand went up, but the pianist kept right on beat, though softer. Preacher Wingate liked to make one last appeal to souls before the final chorus.

"What do you have to dread, friends? Nothing, nothing at all with God Almighty on your side. What do you have to fear? Not even the devil and all his fallen angels, not in this life or the next. Because Jesus is near! Jesus is near! He's near unto you. You draw near unto Him, and He'll take you up in peace just like our good friend Bill Craig. Think about it. Think about it."

Preacher Wingate could always fit what he had to say into the time it took the piano player to run through a verse. Then with his hand held high to heaven as he spoke his last few words, he'd bring it down hard to signal the singing to start again, bringing it down as if he were bringing salvation itself down into the congregation.

Jimmy'd get goose bumps sometimes, at this point in the service. Preacher Wingate was that good at rousing people up. But not now. The hand went down, Jimmy sang, but his flesh stayed smooth as the church folks finished the familiar hymn in the familiar way:

Leaning, leaning, safe and secure from all
alarms;
Leaning, leaning, leaning on the everlasting
arms.

As the women sang "leaning," holding the notes out, the men were able to run underneath them with "leaning on Jesus." In a detached sort of way, Jimmy figured that that little church sure could sing.

Then what had seemed to go on forever ended too soon for Jimmy's taste, and preparations were made to go out to the graveyard. The six pallbearers recessed slowly down the aisle with Mr. Craig, walking as respectfully as a military procession, Preacher Wingate leading the way. Everyone filed out behind them, heading two by two out across the road and into the cemetery.

Once everyone had a chance to gather around the grave, Preacher started the committal service. Jimmy had found his way around to Mildred and some of her family—her mamma and daddy, Uncle Robert, Mildred's sister Liz and her husband.

A cool sun shone down on them, and the air nipped a little, but not too badly. The sky blazed blue, not a cloud in sight. Jimmy's mind wandered. *Pretty day for bad business,* he thought to himself.

The short ceremony passed quickly, and the graveside service came to an end. Jimmy joined the line that would file by the widow and her family, shaking hands and offering words of comfort. Some bent down and spoke quiet assurances; others just silently offered a hand, all the words that needed to be said coming from the eyes. Jimmy stood with Mildred and her family near the end of the line, but finally it dwindled down, and the Holts were just about the only people left. Mildred bent down to offer words of comfort, and then Jimmy found himself standing in front of Mrs. Craig.

The air left him like he had been hit hard on the football field. He stepped up, reached out his hand to Mrs. Craig, and said, "On behalf of Mr. Nordwall, myself, and Ellijay Carpet, I'd like to say how sorry we are for your loss." Those were the best words he could come up with, and he didn't figure they would be well received, given how Mrs. Craig had taken to him the night before. He just had to say them, had to do his job.

She looked down into her lap for a moment. Then, looking up as if waiting for this opportunity, she spoke up loudly enough for everyone still close enough to hear: "Who're you and yore Yankee boss gonna kill next? You ain't sorry a bit. Just one less troublesome old coot to deal with. Ain't that the way of it?"

The implied accusation stunned Jimmy into silence. At last he said simply, "Ma'am, I'm truly very sorry." And then the last thing in the world that he would have expected to happen did happen.

"Now, Margaret," Mildred's mamma said, stepping

up from behind Jimmy and taking the widow woman's hand. "Ain't no sense in talking foolishness." Mrs. Craig glared up for a second, but even in her grief-stricken state, she knew it to be Lois Holt she was talking to.

The wind went out of the old woman's sails. "I don't know, Lois, I don't know what I'm gonna do."

Lois gently pulled Mrs. Craig up out of her chair. "Well, for right now, you're gonna come into the church and eat a bit. We got some good things fixed up, and lots to take home. Don't make a bad time worse by letting bitterness gnaw at your soul. It don't work to the good."

"Reckon yore right," Mrs. Craig said faintly, and Jimmy watched as Lois headed Mrs. Craig off to the church basement, where the food everyone had brought would be spread out.

Mildred hung back with Jimmy. The months of wear and tear on their relationship seemed to get patched up a bit at that moment.

"Jimmy, there wasn't any cause for Mrs. Craig to say those things," she said.

"I don't know," Jimmy said, studying the ground. "Maybe I rode ol' Bill too hard at work. Seems like I was always getting on to him for something or another."

Mildred lifted his head up with her hand and looked him in the eye. "I figure whatever else is true," she said, holding his eye hard, trying to reinforce her words, "you're a fair man, Jimmy Jackson. Can't anyone ask for better than that. I don't know what went on down at the mill between you and Bill, but whatever it was, you didn't cause the wreck. That doesn't even make sense."

"He was drunk," Jimmy said, anguish in his voice. "I heard people at the funeral home saying Bill had been out drinking because it helped him put his workweek behind him." Jimmy thought a minute. "Maybe I drove him to it. Drove him to drink."

"I know you feel bad, Jimmy," Mildred said, conviction in her voice, "but you didn't drive anybody anywhere. You remember that. Bill Craig did what he did. He was his own man, just like you're your own man." A slight smile broke on Jimmy's face. "Of course, you're my man, too," Mildred added, making Jimmy's grin broaden.

"Let's go get something to eat," she suggested, and so she and Jimmy strolled on over toward the church.

Chapter 10

"Yep," Mildred said, "Bill Craig's funeral opened my eyes a bit to what was going on down at the plant." Mildred shook her head. "My word, you could've knocked me over with a feather when Mamma took up for Jim. But she did. And it made me think a little harder about how difficult the new job was on Jim, him having to boss people he'd worked with for years, many of them his friends. I decided then that it probably wasn't a bed of roses.

"Funny thing," Mildred said after looking into her coffee cup, "realizing that people were down on Jim at work made me want to take up for him. Sort of like a mother hen protecting her chicks, I guess. So things got better between us, especially after I heard a little more about what all had been happening at the mill." Mildred reached over and squeezed Caleb's arm. "Bobby's the one who helped me see things straight."

"That's right," Caleb said, "I'd forgotten that Bobby worked at the carpet mill."

"Well, this might come as news to you then," Mildred said. "Part of the reason Bobby got into the car repair business full time was because of all the goings-on at Jim's work. But we'll get to that part of the story a little later."

Thinking about Bobby, Caleb said, "Seems like the whole county came out for Bobby's funeral last year. I still remember what the preacher said: 'This was a man who'd do you proud, no matter what.'"

"So true," Mildred agreed. "And if he said he'd do something, that was the end of the matter. Period."

"Nobody ever did better by his family, either," Joyce said. "He took care of that shell-shocked brother of his like a mother'd take care of a baby. And poor ol' Paul just got worse and worse, so it probably *was* like taking care of a baby at the end. Course he had Miss Stover to help, most of the time. But I still don't see how he did it, him not even twenty years old when his mamma and daddy both died, and with a crippled leg, too."

The Thursday evening after Bill Craig's funeral found Mildred at the Red Dot grocery store. She had driven Jimmy in to work and then taken Johnny and Rachel to spend the day with her folks and Uncle Robert. Jimmy had just called and said to pick him up in a couple of hours—he had to have a meeting with the second shift workers—so Mildred's mamma was keeping the children while she ran to do her shopping for the week.

Mildred was looking over the pork roasts, trying to decide which would make the best Sunday dinner. She had gazed long and hard at the sirloin steaks but decided any meat that cost eighty-nine cents a pound should be saved for a special occasion. Besides, the difference between that and the thirty-nine-cents-a-pound pork would help make up for the dictionary. The Red Dot carried *Webster's Complete and Unabridged Dictionary,* a section per week at eighty-nine cents per section. Jimmy believed the children would need a good dictionary when they started school, and Mildred agreed.

As she turned a roast over, eyeing it carefully, she heard a familiar "clang, clang." She turned around and saw her friend Bobby Ferguson, his leg brace as familiar a part of him now as his quick grin.

"Well, hey there," she said, giving him a welcoming look.

"Well, Mildred Jackson," he replied. "Ain't you the purdiest girl I ever seen picking out a roast."

Mildred smiled. Bobby always had a way of making her feel good about herself. "Aw," she said, "you say that to all the girls."

"Yeah," Bobby acknowledged, "but I only mean it when I say it to you."

They both laughed.

"How's that redheaded cousin of yours?" Bobby asked, referring to Caleb. Caleb and Mildred were cousins, but they had always acted more like brother and sister, and the three of them had been thicker than thieves when they were young. They had run all over Smoky Hollow whenever Mildred came out there to visit, and they'd run all over Ellijay whenever Bobby and Caleb came into town.

Caleb and his daddy, Robert, had lived with Mildred's granny because Caleb's mamma had died young. Once Granny passed on, they'd packed up and moved into Ellijay with Mildred's family. That had happened about a year, maybe less, after Bobby got polio—and that was not too many years before Bobby's folks died and left him in charge of his brother, Paul, who had been shell-shocked in the war.

"Don't hear too awful much from Caleb," Mildred replied to his question. "Just trying to keep up with his studies down in Augusta. Writes often enough, but since he doesn't do much but work and study, not much gets said." She thought a minute and added, "Oh, but there is too some news. Joyce is expecting."

"Well, I'll be," Bobby said. "Reckon the world can put up with another redheaded feller?"

Mildred laughed again. "Suppose it'll have to, if the baby's anything like Caleb. So how are you these days? Brother Paul doin' all right?"

He shrugged. "'Bout the same, I guess. Not any trouble, really. Just has to be watched all the time by somebody."

But Bobby had something on his mind other than ordinary conversation. He stood there lost in thought for a minute, then looked up at Mildred with troubled eyes. "Hey, may not be any of my business, but Mrs. Craig didn't have no cause talking to Jimmy like she did."

"Really?" was all Mildred could muster in reply, knowing that she didn't think it right either, but feeling badly that Mrs. Craig felt the way she did toward her husband.

"Naw," Bobby went on. "Everybody knew Bill Craig would go out and get drunk and play cards every Friday night. Never heard of him hanging one on any other night, just Friday, regular as clockwork. He'd say at work as how it was to get the stink of the workweek out of his system."

Mildred stood there, just nodding her head, wondering where the conversation was headed.

"Way I heard it," Bobby went on, "he got some pretty ugly cards Friday night, which meant he lost most of what he'd earned for the week. Drank even more than usual, they say. Left all mad and high as a kite. That ain't none of Jimmy's doing."

Mildred took it all in, then said, "But Mrs. Craig thought Jimmy drove Mr. Craig too hard. Made him drink more."

"Naw," Bobby said again, his voice full of certainty. "Naw," he said again, like he was buying time, figuring on what all to say.

After he had thoroughly studied a two-pound roast, he looked back at Mildred. "Jimmy tries awful hard to do right by the boss and by all of us that works there." Bobby worked as a mechanic at the mill, keeping the machines in shape. When everything ran like greased lightning, then he'd do odd jobs around the plant. He was good with cars, too, and ran a night and weekend business doing auto repair. He always did a fine job on Jimmy and Mildred's car.

"Went to the office, needed to get a part ordered," Bobby said, looking around to make sure it was just him and Mildred. "Don't like to talk out of school, but as I come up on Nordwall's office, him and Jimmy were carrying on a bit." Bobby gave a guilty grin. "Shouldn't have, don't reckon, but I eavesdropped a mite."

Mildred smiled a little, thinking it was just like Bobby to apologize for something that wasn't really his fault.

Bobby relayed the story. "Anyway, Mr. Nordwall was saying, 'I heard an interesting comment from one of the hands.' And then Jimmy says, 'What was that, Mr. Nordwall?' And Nordwall slapped his desk and leaned in close to Jimmy and said, 'That a mule will work for you for forty years just for the chance to kick you in the head in the end.'"

Bobby paused, letting the mule part sink in. Then he continued, "And then you know what Mr. Nordwall said? Somethin' as how all the workers are like mules, just waiting to kick him and Jimmy in the head. Then Nordwall said a bunch of foolishness like 'stay on your toes,' 'keep the barbarians at the gate,' and 'you and me are in this together—remember.'"

"Well, what was the point of all that?" Mildred asked.

"Just Nordwall's way of trying to make sure which side Jimmy's on." Then Bobby talked on, imitating Mr. Nordwall's voice—"a weasel's voice if I've ever heard one" was what Mildred's mamma had once said. "'You're management, boy, like me. The officers have to run the army, or there'll be no army.'" Bobby rolled his eyes.

"What'd Jimmy say? Anything?" Mildred asked a bit more tentatively than she had meant.

"That's when the row started," Bobby answered. "Mildred, Jimmy let Nordwall know that he stood with the company, but he also said he stood by his workers, too. Jimmy argued 'til he was red in the face about how all the men raised families and went to church and did right as best they could. And that meant working hard, too."

Bobby looked Mildred in the eye. "Jimmy ain't no yes-man. He's a good supervisor. Sure, he wants to please the boss. So what? Helps him make more money. But he don't roll over for him, getting onto people that don't need getting onto."

Bobby thought for a moment. "Reckon it's hard for him these days. It's like Jimmy's walking in two pair of shoes, and he ain't decided which direction to head off in. Can't do it that way forever, though. We'll just have to see how it goes."

Bobby stopped there. Seemed like an opening for a question, so Mildred jumped in.

"Tell me, Bobby. What was really going on between Jimmy and Mr. Craig?"

"Two things, really," Bobby said. "One, ain't nobody works as hard as they can—or should—all the time. Ain't in us."

Mildred generally agreed, though she figured Bobby probably came as close as anyone to doing just that.

"Two, some folks just ain't up to being bossed. Bill Craig didn't like Jimmy bossing him, especially with Jimmy being so much younger. Mildred, I ain't never seen Jimmy get on Bill Craig 'cepting when Bill Craig needed getting on to. But Bill didn't like it, and he got to where he was always in Jimmy's face, causing trouble."

"Mamma said some time back that Mr. Craig was a real good worker."

"Oh, sure," Bobby replied. "But like I said, ain't nobody works their hardest all the time. Jimmy was just doing what I figure a supervisor is there for—supervise. And about everybody reckons Jimmy for fair. Oil and vinegar, though. Jimmy and Bill just didn't seem to mix right proper. But Jimmy bent over backwards to be fair to Bill, and Bill needled Jimmy every chance he got."

Bobby heaved a big sigh and finished up what he had to say. "Anyway, Jimmy ain't got no reason to feel bad, 'cepting as how we all feel bad when somebody passes on. But that's all."

After a little more talk, Mildred picked out a good roast, finished her shopping, and left the store. After she picked the children up, she drove to the mill and got Jimmy. Even though dog-tired, he managed a look of pleasant surprise at the seriousness of his wife's kiss when he got into the car.

Chapter 11

"So," Mildred said, waving off another cup of coffee, "things looked up after my talk with Bobby. Jim and I just went about the business of working and raising a family."

"That's enough, isn't it?" Joyce offered. "Especially when the children are little."

"Lord have mercy," Mildred said. "Sometimes those young'uns just about drove me crazy, especially after Rachel got her legs under her. Between running after her and trying to ride herd on Johnny, I was exhausted."

"Seen lots of young women in my practice over the years," Caleb said, "that seemed a bit sickly, but mostly just needed a good week off."

"I believe that," Mildred replied. "Plus Jim was working himself to death down at the plant. A lot of nights he'd come home and the kids would already be tucked away for the night. Made for hard living, but we did our best."

Joyce nodded. "I know that feeling," she empathized.

"I still remember having little Adam down there in Augusta, Caleb always busy, his last year of school, so he was no help at all. I stayed tired all the time."

"Yep," Mildred agreed, "that was us, too. But, at least it was better than it had been. We'd watch a little television once Jim'd had his supper. I'd take up some knitting or something to have something to do. Never liked just sitting in front of a screen, doing nothing but watching. And Jim'd sit and talk to me during commercials. Or he'd flip through the Sears catalog and talk to me about what he saw."

Mildred got up and found the catalogs she had brought with her. Laying the Christmas catalog aside for the moment, she started thumbing through the 1958 Fall/Winter edition. Caleb and Joyce let her leaf through her memories in silence.

"I could never figure out why," Mildred said after a few minutes, closing the pages and looking at the cover, "why Jim got so caught up in this thing. But he did. Just like a kid in a candy shop—that was Jim and his catalog."

Mildred pushed the book around so Caleb and Joyce could see the front cover better. A kindly-looking older man stood with a group of children—probably meant to be his grandchildren—gazing at all kinds of candy. The man wore a dapper hat and a new-looking gray overcoat, and he carried a bag of groceries in one arm. The other arm draped over the shoulder of a little boy who was also decked out in a brand-new winter coat and cap, complete with fluffy ear flaps. The little boy pointed in wonder at the array of sweets—hard candy, mints, jellied oranges, peppermint sticks, and hard bubble gum.

A little girl, the sister, stood next to him dressed in a bright red winter coat, and her lit-up face showed what she thought. And it was plain for anybody to see that the grandpa stood ready to buy a sack of goodies for his loved ones. Caleb's eye caught the text just above grandpa's haberdashed head:

> Shopping from this catalog…like choosing a favorite candy…is more exciting, more satisfying because there's *extra* variety to please every taste, every budget, every family.

"Let me see here a minute," Mildred said, flipping through the catalog again. "I can even remember him fretting because he thought we weren't gonna get the Christmas catalog." Mildred looked and looked. Finally, she flipped back to the index. "Here it is," she said, "I remember it like yesterday. Even tells the date. Jim thought we'd missed out."

Jimmy sat with his feet up on the coffee table. Mildred generally didn't like to see feet up on the furniture, but, since she and Jimmy had been getting along pretty well lately, she decided to hide her scowl behind the needlework she had in front of her. Besides, having his feet up seemed to relax Jimmy, and Mildred knew he needed some relaxing.

It was Tuesday night, and that meant Western night at the Jackson house. Jimmy had missed *Cheyenne*, but he'd made it home in time to catch *Wyatt Earp*—which he watched mostly to pass the time until *The Rifleman* came on. *The Rifleman* was Jimmy's favorite show. He had even ordered a cap rifle for Johnny from Sears for two dollars and seventy-nine cents. Though it sported a Roy Rogers decal, Jimmy kept telling little Johnny it was the Rifleman's gun. And Johnny seemed to like the idea of being the Rifleman, even though the show came on after his bedtime and he'd never actually seen it. Sometimes on Sunday afternoon, if his daddy wasn't so tired he had to nap all day, Johnny would run around outside, firing his rifle, and his daddy would whirl about shouting, "You got me! You got me!" before falling to the ground.

This evening, though, Jimmy had something other than cowboys on his mind. "Got some nice dresses here," Jimmy said, turning a page of the catalog, saying for about the thousandth time what Mildred had heard well enough the first.

"Yes, Jimmy," Mildred allowed, "some of them are all right." She knew Jimmy was looking at pages eight and nine—he'd showed them to her often enough. "Winter prints," the description read. Women in print dresses in colors like ruby red and sapphire paraded around on the pages with matching hats, handbags, and shoes. One that Jimmy liked—probably because the description, "harem-skirted dress," sounded exotic to him—looked to Mildred like nothing more than a cheap plastic fruit basket plastered on a dress.

She had hurt Jimmy's feelings not too long ago. "Listen," he'd said, reading in a voice filled with something approaching awe. "The Bell Silhouette, young and sophisticated, charmingly fashioned in crisp acetate taffeta." He repeated "crisp acetate taffeta" for effect. Mildred figured he had no clue what that was. He continued,

"Low rounded neckline in back, long back zipper. Pleats and cuff all around skirt; two-inch hem. The new tapered skirt is wide enough for walking."

Mildred nearly doubled over with laughter when she heard that. "Well, how about that? A dress you can walk in!" A tear ran down her cheek, she wiped it off, then she started laughing again. "What'll they think of next? Pants you can work in?" That tickled her even more, so the laughing continued.

Jimmy turned red with embarrassment. "I just thought you could use a nice Sunday dress, something that'd make people sit up and take notice when we come in to church."

"Oh, they'd notice," Mildred went on, catching the red in his face too late. "They'd notice that Mildred Jackson had gone stark raving mad!" Then the laughter poured forth again.

It had taken a bit of cajoling to get Jimmy out of the black mood her laughter had put him in. "Jimmy, I wasn't laughing at you," she said. "I'm just not the sort of girl who wears dresses like that."

"Wouldn't hurt to try," Jimmy had replied, pushing a little.

"Awfully expensive just to try out," Mildred had answered, taking on a serious tone. "Let's not, right now."

That was about as close to a compromise as Jimmy was likely to get—"not now" instead of "absolutely not." So he'd backed off. But now here he was at it again.

Mildred tried to distract him. "Show's on." The quick rifle action and the accompanying "Bang! Bang! Bang!" caught Jimmy's attention. But when the next commercial came up, Jimmy got back to the dresses. Mildred tried again to tell him why they didn't need to buy her a dress-up dress from Sears.

"I like trying them on, seeing how they feel," Mildred explained. "I can go into town to Wright's if I need a new dress." She stopped a moment for emphasis, as if she really contemplated getting a new dress, which she wasn't. "Matter of fact, they have a sale going on right now. Dresses marked down to about ten dollars. You could go with me, and we could see what they have."

Mildred knew pretty much that she had him then. Jimmy loved looking through the Sears catalog. Sometimes she thought he looked less at things like the clothes and instead studied the people wearing them, as if he were trying to figure them out—who they were, and how they got to be in a catalog that everybody in the United States looked at. That kind of looking was a lot more interesting than going down to Wright's, staring at a bunch of dresses that didn't have anybody in them and spending the time waiting while Mildred tried on first this one and then that one.

Jimmy's shoulders slumped a little, and Mildred thought the dress talk would probably stop then. But she wanted to make sure.

"Hey, when do you think the Christmas catalog will get here?" she said. That had been a topic of some discussion already. Jimmy wanted to check out all the new toys, start thinking about Santa Claus. He'd talked about a cowboy outfit for Johnny and maybe some six-shooters to go with his Roy Rogers/Rifleman rifle.

"You know, I've been wondering about that," Jimmy said. "There's a few things here and there about

Christmas in this Fall/Winter catalog, but not much. Thought I read something about it somewhere."

Jimmy began looking through the index, even though the TV show had started up again. He found mention of a few Christmas items in the index, so he flipped to those pages and saw some wrapping paper, a little foil tree, and ornaments. "Wait. Let me look again," he said, going back to the index.

Jimmy's finger ran down the index page. He read out loud: "Christmas Cards…Christmas Decorations… Christmas Kits…Christmas Wrapping Supplies…. Here it is down below all that."

He sat up, taking his feet off the coffee table, posturing himself to make some important announcement. In his best reading voice, he said, "Complete Showing of Christmas Gifts in Sears Special Christmas Catalog to be Mailed about October 20th." Jimmy wore a puzzled expression. "Hey! It should've been here by now."

The Rifleman could've turned into Milton Berle for all the attention Jimmy was paying now to the television. Mildred could tell he was working out the days since October 20.

"Fifteen days," Jimmy proclaimed.

"Well, Jimmy," Mildred said, "it takes a while to mail the catalog from wherever they mail it from. Said it was gonna be mailed October 20, not that you'd get it by then."

"Still," Jimmy worried, "yesterday made two weeks."

"We don't even know if it got mailed when they said it would," Mildred reasoned, wishing she'd never brought the subject up. "Could've been late, for all we know. No use fretting over it."

"Maybe I'll ask around at work, see if anyone else has theirs," Jimmy said. "If your mamma talks to her sister anytime soon, why don't you ask if she's got hers?"

"All right, Jimmy," Mildred replied, not planning on doing anything of the sort. Her mamma'd think she'd gone simple, asking about a silly catalog.

"There's a Sears catalog store down in Canton," Jimmy continued. "Worst case, we could take a drive down there and pick one up, maybe look at some of the new appliances out on the floor." Though the catalog stores didn't really carry much in the way of inventory, they did set out a few big-ticket items to entice the customer.

"We don't need any new appliances," Mildred replied, becoming flustered.

"Oh, I know," Jimmy replied, now lost in his catalog again after having resolved what he saw as a major problem. "We'll just look around a bit, that's all."

"Well, the long and short of it was that the catalog came a few days later, and Jim wore out the pages, quizzing me about the best things for Johnny and Rachel. Shoot, Rachel was barely a year old; she'd have thought a box to play in to be the cat's meow." Mildred pushed aside the Fall/Winter catalog and picked up the Christmas catalog. She ran her hand over the worn cover.

"Jim wanted everything," she said, a look of pain long remembered crossing her face. "It took him a while to find out that there's a price for everything. And that some things are worth it, some not."

A little satisfied smile, a smile that held memories of something good enough to sweep clean the dusty places of the soul, settled on her face.

"He finally found his way," she said. "Took a while, though, and it was a rough road." She laughed. "Between his boss and my mamma, he had a time of it."

Chapter 12

Claude Nordwall sat in his office, pencil in hand, trying to figure out how to meet the quotas. Here it was early November, and some big orders sat on his desk. He had a good idea of the quantity the plant could put out running at full tilt, and he didn't think they could produce enough. They'd miss by a little, but they'd miss. A lot of stores were doing a booming business selling carpet; they pushed it for Christmas and promised delivery and installation before the new year. Thing was, they needed the carpet to meet their promises.

Of course, the old man was the one who'd agreed to all these sales without consulting his sons. Nordwall thought back on the morning's phone conversation with his father.

"I don't know that we can put out that much in the time we've got, not without hiring on." A reasonable thing to say, Mr. Nordwall thought.

"Son," the old man had replied, "I've got to be able

to count on you to do your job. You can do your job, can't you?"

Mr. Nordwall had tried to pull his thoughts together in such a way as to give a stinging reply to his father. The words never came, and the old man had taken the lull in the conversation as hesitation on his son's part.

"Can't you?" the old man asked again.

"Yes, of course I can," Mr. Nordwall finally replied. "It'd go a lot better if we were to pick up some workers, though."

"Absolutely not," the old man said. "You've got to learn to manage your people, son. You've got to establish that you're the boss, and if you say they've got to do more, then they'll do more." Nordwall heard his father heave a heavy sigh over the phone, as if the weight of the world lay upon him and his own son couldn't be counted on to help, not even a little bit. "Claude, are you man enough for this job, or do your mother and I need to send someone down to help you?"

That was all Nordwall needed—his mother dragged into the conversation. "Pop, I can do it," he replied.

"Better hop to it, then," the old man said. "You don't have much time." Then, as usual, old man Nordwall hung up on his son without saying goodbye, assuming the click of the receiver signaled well enough that the conversation had come to an end.

"So, you understand what I need, Jackson?" Mr. Nordwall looked hard at Jimmy, sizing him up, seeing if he was up to the task.

"Yes sir, I do," Jimmy said. "You want me to figure out a way to meet these new production requirements."

"Whoa, Jimmy boy, whoa," Mr. Nordwall said, pushing back his chair and placing his hands on the desk in front of him. He acted as if he were smoothing the top down, the way his hand ran back and across the walnut top. "What I said was that you need to run some ideas by me so I can sort through them as I think through my own plans to meet this production crisis. You just give me a proposal, and I'll give it my fullest consideration," Mr. Nordwall went on, acting as if weighing proposals were his special talent. "Just trying to help you improve as a manager, son." Mr. Nordwall emphasized son, even though he only had about seven years on Jimmy.

So Jimmy spent the next few days trying to remember what he had learned from his business professors, and he stayed up late several nights combing through textbooks and class notes. He'd kept almost everything from his college days.

It only took a day for Mr. Nordwall to approve Jimmy's plan. And so, for the three weeks or so before Thanksgiving, Jimmy became very involved in his new production study. He went around and timed how long it took for individuals and for teams to accomplish their tasks. He timed how long it took to load trucks, how long it took to mat carpet backs, how long it took for each seamstress to sew the same design on kitchen throw rugs.

The workers resisted at first. But then Jimmy convinced them they could be more productive simply by being more aware of how long particular tasks took—plus, he threw in a carrot for them. The incentive part of the plan was the hardest to sell Mr. Nordwall on, but Nordwall finally saw the light and went along with the idea.

"For now, son, for now, let's do it your way, since you've had a big hand in pulling this study together." That's what Nordwall said. Jimmy actually thought of the plan as all his own—Nordwall had done nothing but approve it. But he didn't want to quibble over words, and the boss seemed to have a gleam in his eye as he finally gave the go-ahead for what Jimmy considered to be the jewel of his master plan—rewards.

It took Jimmy about a week to get a baseline on the time needed to complete the various components of the production and shipping process. The following two weeks, workers competed for extra lunchtime. The team that boasted the best times received the next week an extra fifteen minutes for lunch—paid. And the individual that showed the most significant time increase would get off work half an hour early the following Monday. Rewards would come the following week because Jimmy had decided to base his studies on weeklong averages rather than daily averages. He figured it'd be better for production if the increase could be maintained for an entire week rather than just having one really good day and then slacking off because the reward was already won.

The Monday before Thanksgiving, Mr. Nordwall called Jimmy into his office. "Looks like our plan's working, based on the numbers you've supplied, son." Jimmy beamed. Mr. Nordwall went on. "Looks like we'll meet our quotas if we can keep the mill operating at an average of about 95 percent of the best times you've supplied for production." Jimmy again stood silent and proud.

"Something in it for you, son," Mr. Nordwall went on, sounding for all the world like a man so impressed with the work he saw that he couldn't help but appreciate it. "I'm taking a chance, but I think you're worth it."

Mr. Nordwall paused for effect. Jimmy could hardly wait to hear what came next.

"Come with me, son," Mr. Nordwall said, heading for the door.

They walked out to the parking lot. Mr. Nordwall walked over to his parking space, and there sat a brand new Ford Sunliner.

"Nice car, isn't she?" Mr. Nordwall asked, running his hand along the top of the convertible, ending with a pat as if the car were a favored dog.

"She's a beauty," Jimmy agreed.

"Trying her out today," Nordwall went on. "People over at the lot said I could drive it for the day while I made my mind up whether to purchase it or not." Nordwall walked slowly around the car, stopping at each of the tires and giving it a kick.

"Ever hear of a company car?" Mr. Nordwall asked casually.

"Not really," Jimmy replied. There weren't too many companies actually in Gilmer County, just this carpet mill and the hosiery mill where Mildred's dad and uncle worked, a place that had once been a sock mill. He'd been told there might be other carpet plants coming, but so far Ellijay Carpet was the only one.

"Well, now you've heard of it," Mr. Nordwall went on. "Works like this. The company buys a car for the use of its special employees. Employees like you, Jimmy," he emphasized. "They're special. A status symbol. Shows how important you are." Mr. Nordwall lowered his voice, almost conspiratorially low. "Not many people ever get a company car."

Jimmy heart picked up a pace, his face flushed.

"Here's how it works," Mr. Nordwall repeated. "The company buys the car, owns the car. That's why it's called a company car. But you get to drive it, as long as you make the payments." Nordwall let that part settle in for a minute. "You make the payments," he repeated, "but the company owns the car until you've made them all. Understand? That's because the company will buy it from the dealership. Then, for the price of monthly payments—stretched out so it doesn't cost you so much, so you can afford it—you get the use of the car. And when it's paid off—then it's yours!"

Jimmy thought on that for a minute, trying to puzzle out how this was a better deal than buying his own car, but Nordwall jumped in before he could think for too long.

"See, the company buys the car. That means you don't have to have a down payment, you don't have to meet the bank's credit standards. Shows you're special, shows the company considers you trustworthy. You don't need collateral, you don't need cash. Your good name, your good standing with the company—that's all it takes. And payments are extended over a longer period of time, so you don't pay as much each month, either. Not nearly as much."

Nordwall closed in for the kill. "Here, son," he said, "take the keys. Go for a spin. See if this isn't the kind of car you deserve." Jimmy hesitated. Nordwall added, "You've earned it." Jimmy started to take the keys, but Nordwall pulled them back.

"It's just a little ride now," he said. "After Thanksgiving, on Friday, we'll make it official. Got a little something to talk over with you then. We'll sign some papers, talk about how we're going to keep this production schedule up, then the car's yours."

Nordwall handed over the keys. As Jimmy opened the door and slid behind the wheel, new car smell all around him, Mr. Nordwall reached down and patted his shoulder. "Good job, son."

And then…what a feeling, driving the company car to the town square and back.

It wasn't just a smooth ride. Jimmy floated on air.

Chapter 13

"That," Uncle Robert proclaimed, "was a Thanksgiving dinner." He pushed back from the dining table, and a polite yet acknowledging belch made its way out. Polite because it sounded none too loud, acknowledging because everybody at the table had had their fill and more. They'd had themselves a feast, and none of them thought it a crime to let it be known—within reason—just how nice and full their bellies were.

The smell of food hung heavy over all the feasters. If it had been the smell of ether, nobody would've been more drowsy. Now came the time for relaxing, small talk, and droopy eyelids. No one would take offense if, when they'd all moved to the living room, a little snore escaped instead of a reply to some question that didn't really need answering anyway.

Mildred's daddy, Henry, her uncle Robert, and Jimmy all left the table, taking their sweet tea with them. Mildred took Rachel and Johnny into her old room and settled them for a nap. Even Johnny, who napped only sporadically these days, fell asleep right away, so Mildred returned to the kitchen to help her mamma clean up. Kitchen talk revolved around Mildred's sisters, Liz and Becky, who had spent the day with their in-laws, and Jimmy's mamma and brothers, who'd been invited over to Jimmy and Mildred's that evening for dessert, as well as the comings and goings of other friends and neighbors and family.

The conversation lasted longer than the cleanup chores. The leftovers were quickly stored away and all the dishes washed—though a few found themselves back on the dining table, near the cakes and pies, so people could have an additional bite of something sweet if the notion took them. Mildred and Lois wiped their hands, hung up their aprons, and made their way into the living room.

Henry Holt sat in his big overstuffed chair, feet propped up, pipe hanging from his mouth. Mildred always thought the pipe suited her daddy. It made him look thoughtful, which she knew him to be. It also kept his mouth occupied, so that he could go an entire afternoon in conversation with his wife with just the occasional nod and the obligatory "hm-hmm" to show he stood in agreement with about everything she had to say. If Mildred had been asked to sum up, in just a couple of words, what her house was like on an average Sunday afternoon—or on a special day like Thanksgiving, with everyone home from work and not fretting about chores that needed to be done—she would've said those lazy afternoons slid along on the sound of her mamma's voice and the smell of her daddy's tobacco.

Uncle Robert sat in a rocking chair, one that had

been around for as long as Mildred could remember. She could picture her old granny, passed on now some sixteen years come Christmas, rocking in that chair. Or see herself as a child, when Granny was up and about in the kitchen, sneaking up into that chair and rocking until somebody came along and told her to get out of it. Granny's chair was one of the pieces of furniture Uncle Robert had brought with him when he and cousin Caleb moved in with Mildred's family. Now he sat rocking and passing the time by engaging in one of his favorite activities—sitting and reading aloud to anyone who was interested from the Ellijay *Times-Courier.*

"Got us a regular crime spree going on, reckon," he was saying as the ladies made their way into the room. Lois eased herself into the high-backed formal chair she had reupholstered and restuffed any number of times now. She'd worn it out from years of use, but she liked it so much she'd never even considered replacing it. Last time around, even the springs had been replaced, which meant the chair didn't sit as comfortably as it used to. But Lois, doggedly determined, figured she could wear those springs down to something approaching coziness.

Jimmy was across the room, stretched out on the sofa as much as he could without actually lying down. "How's that?" he asked Robert.

"Says here a feller broke into Cox Drug Store," Robert replied. "Broke into the doctor's office 'fore that."

"Ain't hardly been nothing in that paper but bad news lately," Lois put in. "Never seen nothing like it in my life."

"What've we had now, four straight weeks of crime?" Henry asked.

"Yep," Robert answered, everyone knowing him to be the authority on what the paper said. "Started with that principal charged with stealing money from the school."

"Lunch money, right?" Mildred asked.

"Yep," Robert said. "Imagine a feller who's s'posed to be educating young'uns stealing their lunch money. Course, paper said he was skimming money from the lunch fund. Same thing, though. Like taking a littl'un's dinner pail."

"Ain't right," Lois said, stating the obvious but with such conviction that it sounded like the thunder of judgment.

"What else has been going on?" Jimmy asked. "Been too busy to pay much attention to the paper."

"Terrible things," Robert went on. "Week after the principal was caught, paper ran an article on a rape right here in Ellijay. Feller was from up in Tennessee, but still, ain't right."

"Nope," Lois answered. "And then there was that awful thing with the McClure woman."

"What awful thing?" Jimmy asked.

"Killed by her husband," Lois put in. "Her only thirty-seven, and that crazy feller shot her."

"He's dead now, too," Robert said. "Shot himself after he shot her. Paper says he died about a week later."

"Good," Lois said. She started to speak her mind about how she hoped he suffered good and long while he lay dying, but Mildred had had enough talk of crime.

"Isn't there something else more interesting in that paper? Leastways nicer, this being Thanksgiving."

"Well, there's something kinda interesting here," Robert said, folding back the paper. "Georgia Power advertisement. Dangdest thing you've ever seen." Of course, Uncle Robert wasn't about to turn the paper over to anyone else quite yet, so he read the ad to them.

"Says here, 'Breakfast time—1962?' There's this great big metal lamp-looking thing, cone shaped. A woman's got bacon frying underneath it. All dressed up doing her cooking in heels and pearls." Robert looked up from the paper at Lois. "How come you don't ever cook in heels and pearls?" He and Henry both laughed.

Lois cast a disdainful look at Robert and Henry. "Reckon I could cook buck naked for all you two would notice, so long as you got your fill of food that's better'n either of you deserve."

Mildred let out a giggle at her mother's risqué comment. Robert sniggered. "Well, anyway, says here that cooking'll just take seconds. Uses high-frequency radio waves. Won't need no frying pan; just do it on a paper plate. Cooks just the food."

"Well, you see who that advertisement's for then, don't you?" Lois said. "The paper plate crowd. If you ain't gonna use real plates, don't much care if what you serve is any good."

"Just saying," Robert continued, "the future's right around the corner. Says here that Georgia Power's gonna be there to supply all our electrical needs."

"Reckon we'll continue to meet their monetary needs," Henry said, chuckling.

"Reckon so," said Robert, shaking his head.

"Hey, look here," Robert said, this time really interested in what he saw. "Says *The Ten Commandments* is coming to the theater. December three through nine."

"They say it's awful good," Lois declared, repeating what her sister Doris had told her. Doris hadn't actually seen it herself, but she had friends who'd driven down to Marietta to see it.

"Got Yul Brenner and Charlton Heston," Robert said, reading aloud. "'An absolute must! Share it with your whole family!' Well, now, that's a good idea. We orta all go when it comes."

They all mulled over if Charlton Heston might make a good Moses or not. Robert went on through the paper and was folding it up to put it away when something caught his eye in the lower left corner of the front page.

"Hey, Mildred," he said, "we're in the paper."

"Who? Me and you?"

"Naw, not really," Robert said, "but in a way we are. Says here, 'All-night service at Talona Baptist Church on Saturday night. Services start at seven-thirty. Refreshments served at midnight.' Now, here's the part with us: 'Several singers and quartets invited for the night.' Reckon that means us."

"I almost forgot about that," Mildred said. "We talked about adding a new song to our routine. We still gonna do that?"

"Reckon we can," Robert said. "Want the paper, Henry?" Mildred's daddy took the paper as Robert got out of the rocker. He headed back to his room and came back with his guitar.

"Heard a real nice way of doing an old favorite," he said. He handed the guitar to Mildred, grabbed a straight-backed chair from the dining room, and set it next to Mildred, taking the guitar from her. A piece of paper had been neatly folded and inserted between the strings. Robert pulled it out, ran his hand across it to flatten it out, and handed it to Mildred.

"Has a nice, upbeat, toe-tapping rhythm," Robert said. "It's a song about death, but it has to do with joy, too, like expecting good things to come."

Robert wrapped his worker's hand around the neck of the guitar, forming a D-chord. He started a pick and strum, four-four time. "See if you don't like this," he said as he started to sing.

> To Canaan's land I'm on my way,
> Where the soul never dies.
> My darkest night will turn to day,
> Where the soul never dies.

"Like that?" Robert asked, still strumming. Mildred nodded. "If you think you've got it, go ahead and join in on the chorus. Let's just do unison right now. No harmony." Mildred started singing with Robert.

> No sad farewells,
> No tear-dimmed eyes,
> Where all is love,
> Where the soul never dies.

Robert picked and strummed a little longer. Then he said, in a voice made a little sad by memories of Thanksgivings past, back when somebody else filled the rocking chair he'd been sitting in a few minutes ago, "Mamma would've liked this verse."

A rose is blooming there for me,
Where the soul never dies.
And I will spend eternity,
Where the soul never dies.

Mildred joined in on the chorus again, this time trying out the harmony and stretching out the third line to say "peace and joy and love."

"That's what everybody's used to," she said, and Robert nodded.

By the time they had gone through the song for about the third time, they had it down, and even Lois sat there tapping her foot in rhythm with the song.

"We can practice some more later," Robert said. "I just wanted to see if you liked it or not." He stood and picked up his guitar. "Plus, can't sing too much on this full stomach. Need me a little tea to help it digest."

"I'll take a little of that tea," Lois said as he walked past her.

Robert turned and placed a hand on Lois's chair, bending over near her face. "Whatcha got to say?" Robert teased.

He knew better, of course. While most folks might have said "please" just to get the tea faster, Lois just looked at him. "If you don't get me my tea, you ain't ever gonna eat another morsel of food in this house again, most of which comes your way without a single solitary please."

Robert laughed and patted his sister's shoulder. "Well,

some folks would take that as an idle threat, but I know better." He turned to go put up his guitar and get two glasses of tea. "Course, most folks don't have a sister that'd make a rattlesnake seem accommodating."

Everyone laughed at that one, including Lois. And recognizing a good zinger when she heard one, and knowing it wasn't often that Robert was able to one-up her, she held her tongue in appreciation for words well spoken, though obviously wrongheaded.

"Seen the new cars, Jimmy?" Henry asked, the paper open on his lap.

"Yes, I have," Jimmy said. He sounded emphatic for somebody who hadn't had time to keep up with the paper.

"Look mighty fine," Henry continued. "'Here's what makes the fifty-nine Fords the world's most beautifully proportioned cars,'" Henry read, imitating Robert's way of reciting from the paper. He turned the paper around so Jimmy could see the pictures. A Thunderbird, a Fairlane 500, and the new Country Sedan (nine passengers) seemed to gleam on the page, insofar as black and white newsprint can make anything gleam. But Jimmy reached over and pointed to the fourth vehicle.

"That's the car." He said it as if he were making an announcement. His finger touched on the paper, and beneath his fingertip lay "The new Ford Sunliner."

"A convertible?" Henry asked. His voice made it sound as if the notion were a bit shocking.

"A convertible," Lois said with less shock, more contempt. "What danged fool would want a convertible?" It wasn't really a question, more of a statement of fact.

Robert walked back in, gave his sister her tea with a

bow, and grabbed the dining-room chair and put it back where it belonged. He set his tea down so he could cut himself just the smallest piece of pecan pie. Being polite, he asked, "Anybody else want some pie?" And at almost the same exact time, Jimmy blurted out, "I would."

"You want pie?" Robert asked, a little befuddled, wondering how Jimmy knew he was going to ask that question.

"Uh, no thank you, Robert," Jimmy said, sounding all of a sudden a bit too formal. He sat up straight, and Mildred let out a sigh as she realized what was about to be said. She started fishing around for something to say, hoping to divert a conversation that she knew wouldn't go anywhere good. But she was too late.

"I'd like to have a convertible," Jimmy said. Mildred saw that he wore his arguing face, his lower jaw jutting out slightly, his eyes narrowed, like he needed to focus better on whoever it was he was about to have a fuss with.

"Lord have mercy," Lois said. "What would you want with a convertible? More trouble than they're worth. I hear they're cold in winter, and they can't keep the rain out." Lois gave Jimmy one of her "have you gone simple in the head?" looks. "Riding with the top down is just dandy on a summer's day with some fine sunshine." She paused for emphasis. "But life ain't all sunshine, son. You need something solid to help you weather the storm."

"Life ain't all gloom and doom, either," Jimmy replied, heat rising in his voice. "What's the point of working your whole life without a little something for pleasure?"

"Pleasure?" Lois broke in. "Only pleasure worth having in life comes in the form of what you got sitting here in this living room with you. Family. Take pleasure in your family, Jimmy. Don't go looking to cars for that. A car is to get you where you're going, hoping the whole time that the thing don't get a flat and the engine don't overheat."

Mildred hung her head. She knew what was about to overheat, and it didn't have anything to do with automobiles.

"Reckon the real pleasure in life is knowing you've done your best by your family," Jimmy said, a smoldering anger evident in his voice. "And I reckon it'd be nice to have two cars, like some folks, like the ones who seem to run things around this town."

"Oh, Jimmy," Lois said, "ain't no use getting all bothered. 'Less you went and got yourself a money tree, don't figure you can afford two cars anymore'n the rest of us."

By now Jimmy heard every word out of Lois's mouth as if she were a mamma trying to reason with her little boy. But he wasn't little, and he wasn't her boy, so in he jumped with both feet.

"Well, just so happens I've got more going my way than you think," Jimmy told her. "Already made arrangements for a car, a new Sunliner just like the one in the paper." He crossed his arms, fell back into the sofa, and dared anyone to ask any more about it. Of course, Lois started to, but she was cut off by Mildred.

"What do you mean you've made arrangements for a car?" Mildred asked. She came up out of her chair, hands on her hips, looking enough like her mother to cause most folks to think carefully about what to answer next.

"Great," Jimmy huffed, standing up again himself. "Can't a man surprise his wife once in a while? I'll drive the new car back and forth to work, and you can have our old one to do your running around without having to take me to work."

"Oh, nice surprise for me, eh?" Mildred asked. "I get the old car, you get the new. Fine. Don't make it sound like a big surprise for me, though. Sounds more like something for you."

"It's not that way," Jimmy said, voice getting louder. "It's a company car, that's all. That's why I have to drive it back and forth to work. You can drive it on weekends, or us together."

"A company car?" Mildred and Lois asked together, looking at each other and then at Jimmy.

About then Henry said, "Seems the civilized thing to do is to sit back down, unless y'all plan on throwing punches." Henry had lived a long time with Lois, and he was a man who knew how to let the water roll off his back, so to speak. But what was happening looked like it might turn ugly. He saw no use in that.

Lois turned on her husband, starting to speak her piece to him. But before the words came out, Robert put in, "Henry's right. Ain't no use acting this way. Besides," he continued, "this is something for Mildred and Jimmy to talk about. Don't need to be aired out right here in the living room. Not on Thanksgiving." Robert and Henry together carried enough quiet authority that the steam blew out of Mildred and Jimmy, and they both sat down.

Lois took a bit longer to cool off. "Don't tell me to be civilized," Lois grumbled. "I'm just talking, that's all. No need to act as if we ain't got the sense God gave us. Ain't none of us fighting, are we?" she asked. "Course we ain't fighting." She looked crossly at Henry, then at Robert. "Just talking," she emphasized again, straightening herself up in her very straight chair.

"It's simple," Jimmy continued. "I got something started at work, my idea, and it panned out." Jimmy looked over at Mildred. "Remember the study I set up?" Mildred shook her head up and down, acknowledging that she'd heard that part but not a word more, especially not about a new car.

"A reward, that's what this is—for a job well done." Jimmy crossed his arms. "A reward I deserve. Don't talk about what you don't know about."

Lois looked over Jimmy's way and said, "That's awful big talk, son. Remember, the Bible says pride goes before a fall."

Jimmy curtly replied, "Ain't nobody gonna fall."

"So, there we sat," Mildred said, hands up in exasperation, "having had a good meal and sung a nice song, when Mamma and Jim went at each other."

"So, how'd it end up?" Joyce asked.

Mildred frowned. "That was the only Thanksgiving of my whole life that I didn't feel very thankful. Mamma had some more words with Jim that made him so mad that he stormed out, and of course the children and I had to leave when he left."

"What'd she say?" Joyce asked.

"Oh, it was just Mamma at her usual best. Jimmy

ended up trying to explain the deal on the company car, how it all worked. Sounded like foolishness to Mamma, and it sounded more than just a little suspicious to me, I have to admit."

Mildred stretched her neck as if she were trying to work out a kink. Joyce found herself wondering if the telling of the story, which had become a full evening's affair, was Mildred's way of working a little kink out of her memory, smoothing out her recollections of her life as a wife, which had come and gone too soon. Never mind that she'd been married a good forty years. In a good marriage, that didn't matter. Forty years didn't seem that much longer than four.

"I remember Jim saying, 'Look, Lois, the way this company car works just makes good business sense. I can't help it if you don't understand business.'"

"Ha!" Caleb let out. "Aunt Lois didn't let that one go by."

"No," Mildred replied, "her answer was quick, and I'm afraid it hit close enough to the truth that it hurt Jim to have to hear it."

"What'd she say?" Caleb asked.

"Oh, the usual Mamma thing." Mildred took on her mamma's voice and demeanor, repeating the words that had so wounded her husband those many years before. "Young man, ain't no way something makes good business sense when it just plain don't make good horse sense. Use your head, son. This car may be about a whole lot of things, but one thing it ain't about: good sense."

Mildred paused, then declared, "That was a bad day, followed by too many more."

Chapter 14

Jimmy woke extra early the Friday after Thanksgiving. Things had been cool between Mildred and him after getting home from her mamma's, but that was a pattern that had developed over the course of the fall. Things got bad; things got better. Jimmy counted on riding the ups and downs until things fell out his way at work, then everyone would see he'd been right all along, Mildred's mamma included. Jimmy was determined to make a better life for his family, whether they knew it was best for them or not. They'd come around. That confidence, plus the expectation of receiving the first real symbol of his new status at work—a company car—put a whistle on his lips. The extra money from his promotion was good, but now he'd have something for everyone to see and admire, even if he had to pay for it out of that extra money.

But a little something nagged at him. He had left Mildred without kissing her goodbye. Even in bad times, there was always at least a perfunctory kiss. Jimmy knew that to be a part of his marriage, and he made sure it got done, like all the other things he took care of. His family mattered to him, and he put effort into making sure it looked like a family to be proud of.

But this morning—well, he had gotten up especially early, and the children were usually up at sunrise, so Mildred never got to sleep in. He'd told himself she needed what sleep she could get, so he'd just do her a favor and not wake her. He'd just get his own breakfast and run on and have a good start.

And that really was the snag, because there was another reason he didn't kiss Mildred. She knew it was company car day, and if she woke up, she might have something to say about that, and Jimmy wanted to be able to enjoy his anticipation without anyone casting sideways glances or intimating that something wasn't just right. So he let her sleep, but not really for the reason he told himself. And deep inside, he knew himself the poorer for it. Maybe that's why the jolly tune on his lips didn't really sound all that jolly. Anyway, he couldn't keep it up. After just a few minutes on the road, the whistle faded away.

As Jimmy pulled into the mill lot, he noticed the Sunliner down the way, where Mr. Nordwall pretty much parked by himself. Mr. Nordwall's gleaming Cadillac was there, too, even this early in the morning.

Jimmy pulled into a space and turned the engine off. Sitting by himself, he looked over at the shiny convertible. He got a good picture of it in his mind's eye, and then he closed his eyes, seeing the car with him in the driver's seat. And he wasn't just driving. He was parking, and he was doing it in a space all to himself, apart from everybody else. He was the boss—no, the owner. He'd be the owner one of these days. It'd be hard work, but he could see himself doing it, because he could see himself in the car in the right parking space.

Jimmy finally opened his eyes and stepped out of the car. He let out one breath, then two. He inhaled deeply and then exhaled, emptying his lungs. Then, with an air of confidence mingled with excitement, he walked to the entrance. By the time he got there, he was stepping lively—despite his limp—and felt like a man on top of life. He grabbed the door handle and, for that second, he felt like he was walking into a new world.

Jimmy made his way to Mr. Nordwall's office. He stopped and knocked, half peering in as he did so. Mr. Nordwall looked up and motioned Jimmy to come in.

"Good morning, sir," Jimmy said, rocking a little bit on the back of his heels just because he had such a hard time keeping still.

"Well, I think it might turn out that way," Nordwall said. "I think what we've worked up is going to play out just right." Nordwall looked down again at pages on his desk that seemed to have all sorts of numbers. After a quick finger ran down one column, Nordwall looked back up and said, "Ready for your car?"

"Yes, sir," Jimmy replied.

"Let's go, then," Nordwall said, pushing away from the desk and getting up with a slowness of a man fifteen years older. Jimmy sometimes thought Mr. Nordwall didn't appear to be the healthiest person he'd ever met, and it seemed sitting suited him better than getting up and moving around.

"I think you're going to like this," Nordwall said

as they made their way out the door and moved to the shiny Sunliner.

Jimmy could hardly keep from walking faster than Mr. Nordwall's old-man pace. As they got to the car, Jimmy noticed that it was parked a couple of feet from the curb. Mr. Nordwall took him by the arm and steered him into position beside the car so that he could see between the curb and the front of the car.

"Look there, son, and see what hard work does for you," Mr. Nordwall said. Jimmy's eyes ran across the white paint that shone brand-new against the dark asphalt. The letters soaked into his brain like rain on parched earth:

JIMMY JACKSON
SUPERVISOR

As Jimmy stared at his own personal parking space, he heard a rattle of keys. "Here, son, these go in your pocket now." Jimmy reached for them. He automatically looked heavenward, as if driven instinctively to offer a prayer for such a good thing. But before long, Mr. Nordwall said, "Let's go sign a few papers—just formalities." And then Mr. Nordwall steered Jimmy back into the office, where Jimmy signed loan papers, not really noticing that they carried an interest rate higher than what the bank charged.

Not more than an hour passed before Mr. Nordwall entered the working part of the mill, where the carpet actually got made. This in itself was an unusual occurrence. The building had been built so that a rather long hallway separated the business offices from the main part of the plant. Since Jimmy's promotion, the boss had rarely ventured down that hallway. Only a few people in shipping, who needed to coordinate deliveries, and Bobby, who had to order parts and supplies, saw Mr. Nordwall on a regular basis.

Today, though, Mr. Nordwall indicated to Jimmy that he needed to make a quick announcement for the whole plant to hear, so Jimmy rounded everyone up. They stood expectantly in the quiet building—eerie in a way because they were all used to the noise of making carpet. Mr. Nordwall reached up, tugged at his tie for no apparent reason, and then made a relatively short announcement.

"Because of Jimmy Jackson's work, we now know what to expect from our workers."

Jimmy, standing beside the boss, wondered for a second why Mr. Nordwall was fronting him. That wasn't like Mr. Nordwall, who all along had talked about the production study as if he himself had come up with it and just sent Jimmy out to do the grunt work.

"New production quotas will now be posted for each week," Mr. Nordwall continued. "It's important that we reach these goals to meet the Christmas demand. We now know, because of Jimmy Jackson's work, the times for the most efficient workers. And we know not everyone works at the same speed. Therefore, we have based these quota goals on a work rate of 95 percent efficiency. All of you— " Mr. Nordwall emphasized the *you* "—must work to meet the minimum efficiency rate of 95 percent of peak. Our own good Mr. Jackson will continue to monitor your work. Anyone who doesn't meet this new requirement will be dismissed without notice."

Mr. Nordwall hesitated, licked his dry lips, and the pause gave the workers just enough time to start to react to this news. Hints of angry words floated up toward Jimmy and Mr. Nordwall, who shifted nervously, obviously wanting nothing to do with an unpleasant situation.

He glanced over to Jimmy. Then he proclaimed before walking back to his office, "Any questions about this new policy may be directed to the head of the production study, Mr. Jackson."

At that moment Jimmy did walk into a brand-new world—hell. When he left that place, finally, at the end of a day he thought might last forever, he went home in his new Sunliner. By then, however, the excitement from that morning had long since evaporated.

He parked in his regular parking place at home, realizing for the first time that he'd have to go back with Mildred over the weekend to collect their old car. Climbing out of the gleaming Sunliner, he turned around and glared at it.

He didn't even try to get Mildred to come out and see the new car.

"One of the worst parts about the way things fell out at the plant, after that awful day when Mr. Nordwall took Jim's ideas and seemed to turn them around on him in a way Jim would never have done, came about a week later," Mildred said. Joyce and Caleb sat around tsk-tsking as Mildred recounted what Jim had said went on at the mill the day he had gotten the new car, a day he didn't tell her about until after things had gotten patched up between them. But Mildred knew something was wrong at the time, just from the way Jim acted.

"So Mr. Nordwall took Jimmy's ideas and used them in a way Jimmy never would have done," Mildred said. "And Jimmy had to take the heat for it all. But the worst of it," she added, "came about a week later."

"What happened then?" Caleb asked.

"He had to fire his brother Harold."

"That couldn't have been pleasant," Joyce said.

"No," Mildred agreed. "I think it was a little hard all along, big brother bringing in little brother and being his boss and all. But there never was much sign of trouble until the firing."

"Harold didn't meet his quota?" Caleb prodded.

"No," Mildred replied, "and from what I could gather, it was a deliberate thing. Harold got right in his face—said he wasn't some danged machine that you could punch a number into and expect him to spit out just the right amount of work."

"He did it just to test Jim," she added. "And it *was* a test, I'm telling you. Maddest I'd ever seen old Mrs. Jackson."

Chapter 15

An early Saturday morning caught Mildred looking out her window at the coming of a December rain. The temperature stood at about thirty-eight degrees, and the clouds showed no sign of letting the sun through. In fact, Mildred thought it grayer now than when she had first gotten up.

She hadn't slept much the night before. Waking from what was, at best, a fitful nap—and that before the chickens even had a chance to get up and stir—she'd decided to go ahead and get up rather than lie in bed with a husband who had hardly spoken more than two rude words to anybody the night before. She knew things were bad at work; she'd heard the talk. But things weren't much better at home.

She poured herself a cup of hot coffee, though she didn't know how much good it would do against the coming wet cold. She stepped out of the kitchen and looked out the picture window in the living room. About then, the sheets of gray in the sky let loose sheets of gray that fell to the ground. From the looks of it, Mildred counted on an all-day rain. She didn't relish the situation—cooped up in the house with the children and a husband who hadn't made for fit company since Thanksgiving dinner.

Suddenly, a sharp rap at the kitchen door made her jump. She didn't move at first—how could anyone be knocking at the door at such an early hour? Then a more insistent banging started, one that let the householders know there was no ignoring the door.

Mildred turned and moved slowly toward the kitchen. Lack of sleep made her motions feel heavy, as if she were walking through water. About then, she heard noise back in the hallway, and from the rustling around she knew Jimmy had gotten up. She turned around just in time to see him coming down the hallway, tying together his housecoat. He looked up with an expression of dissatisfaction. "Only morning I get to sleep in," he grumbled as he joined her in the kitchen. "What's going on?" He said it as if, whatever it was, it was somehow Mildred's fault.

She responded in kind. "Don't have any idea, but since you're up, you can get that door."

But before Jimmy could open the door, the visitor banged so hard Mildred thought the pane might break. The rattling irritated Jimmy, so he left his hand on the knob without unlocking the door and pushed back the little curtain to peer out and see what—or who—this was all about.

"Ahhh, not this early," Jimmy moaned as he stomped his foot. Mildred knew Jimmy well enough to know frustration was already boiling over in him even before he let the visitor in. Mildred herself did a double take as Jimmy's mamma pushed in through the barely open door. Her white hair shone with the raindrops. She must have stepped out of her car just as the heavens opened up.

Mrs. Jackson took only two quick steps into the kitchen—just out of the doorway good—before she lit into her son. Mildred opened her mouth to offer her mother-in-law some of the freshly brewed coffee, but then the old lady stomped her foot hard on the floor. And if Jimmy's stomping had been a sign of frustration, Mildred knew Mrs. Jackson did it out of pure fury.

"How could you do this?" Mrs. Jackson barked out even before Jimmy had the door closed.

"Mamma, he wasn't doing his job."

Mildred stepped over to the cabinet and pulled down coffee cups, thinking they might be needed at some point. She didn't know what else to do, so she just stood there while Jimmy's mamma really let loose.

"How in the world could you do this to your own family?" Mrs. Jackson demanded. "How about me? All I get is what Harold brings in to help out and the sale of timber that Harold and Billy look after, now that you're too busy to see after your own mamma." A grimace passed over Jimmy's face as she said that.

Jimmy started to break in, to remind his mamma of all the things he looked after around her house. But she blustered on.

"Family, Jimmy, family. Ain't you ever heard about taking care of family first?"

Jimmy tried to defend himself. "Like I said, mamma, he just wasn't doing his job."

"How could he?" she spat back. "All these new rules and regulations that you've thought up, making yourself look all high and mighty while it's people like Harold that do the work. Living off the backs of others—that's what you're doing."

Those words got Jimmy's hackles up. "I work as hard or harder than anybody in that whole plant, Mamma. Harder and longer. Don't tell me I'm mooching off the work of any man."

Jimmy's mamma changed tactics—a change for the worse. "Your daddy'd be ashamed of you, boy."

That set off a chain reaction that, despite her efforts to interrupt, appeared to Mildred to break the ground between mother and son, a chasm too wide to ever be bridged. Years of hurt and embarrassment came rumbling out of Jimmy like a volcano erupting, and there was no saving the mountaintop. Mildred knew it was bad. Once Jimmy started in, he barreled over his mother's objections, getting louder and louder, drowning out everything she had to say as he spoke his mind.

"Ashamed of me? Ashamed of me?" Jimmy's eyes bulged in his red face. "Don't talk to me about my daddy being ashamed of me. I'm not the one running moonshine. I'm not the one can't make an honest living. I'm not the one," he ran on, voice pitching higher and higher, "thrown in jail and finally killed by a bunch of no-goods from Dawsonville serving time for the same danged crime." Jimmy stopped long enough to catch his breath. His voice lowered. "I'm not the one to ruin any chance of my son making a better life for himself. My boy will never be called home on account of me and my doings. Never. Don't talk about my daddy being ashamed of me."

"Your daddy and me," Mrs. Jackson said, a quiet dignity having fallen on her now, "we done our best to raise you young'uns, done it the best we could, and we didn't do so bad, either. You got this land your house sets on because your daddy left it to you. What you got, you got because of him." Mrs. Jackson met her son's eyes with a level glare. "So don't you ever talk about your daddy like that again. Not in my presence." Gathering up the dignity that had fallen about her, Mrs. Jackson said in a formal voice, "Goodbye," and walked out the door.

Jimmy had to have the last word. "Land's the only good thing I ever got," he yelled as his mother made her way through the rain. She didn't run or trot or seem to take any notice at all that the rain fell on her in bucketfuls. As she opened the car door, Jimmy yelled out, "I pay for this house. I pay the taxes. I pay for everything in here. Don't tell me what I have comes from anybody but me." But by the time he had finished the car door had closed. Mrs. Jackson turned the car around and headed home.

"So a bad time got worse," Mildred said, thinking back on that rainy, gray day.

"A whole lot worse?" Joyce asked.

Mildred nodded. "Storm broke out something fierce," she replied. "And where there's thunder, I reckon, there's gonna be lightning."

Mildred stood dazed, coffee cup still in hand, a look of confusion on her face. "You fired Harold?"

The question that got asked wasn't the question that got heard. Jimmy heard only accusation.

"Don't start with me," he said sharply.

"I'm not starting anything," Mildred retorted. "And if you can't handle a simple question, then you need to go cool down. Nobody talks to me that way in my own kitchen."

"Your kitchen?" Jimmy asked, incredulity and sarcasm dripping from his voice. "Who pays for *your* kitchen?"

"Don't start down that road," Mildred said. "Why don't you go take a shower, take time to get off your high horse, then come back when you can talk civil?"

"Don't tell me what to do," Jimmy said, his throat tightening, "like I'm a snot-nosed kid you can order around."

Mildred stepped toward Jimmy. Her voice played level, dangerously level. "Jimmy Jackson, you will not talk to me like that."

"Quit telling me what to do!" Jimmy snapped. His head pounded, and his heart beat fast enough he should've been running. Everything at the mill, all the good things gone wrong, bright ideas turned into dismal, push-your-nose-to-the-grindstone policies, hopes for a better life that turned the present one into sheer misery, pushed on the inside of his head so badly he thought it would blow right off his shoulders. And with all that exploding in his head, he didn't have the slightest moment to consider what he did next. He raised his arm, hand open, as if he stood on the brink of slapping his wife. And by the time he realized what he had done and brought his hand back down, it was too late.

Instead of backing up at the sight of possible violence at the hand of her husband, Mildred pushed forward right into him, standing toe to toe, chest to chest with him, looking up into his eyes. He started to stammer something as he brought his hand down, but the sound stuck in his throat as Mildred's words hit him like a sledgehammer in the stomach.

"Don't you ever," she said, words hard as iron, "raise your hand to me again."

Jimmy again tried to say something. The look in his wife's eyes punched all the wind out of him. In a low voice, almost a whisper, he started to say he was sorry. But whatever had lifted him up in his rage had dropped him just as quickly, and the energy that had radiated from him just moments ago seemed to have simply burned him up in its heat, and he felt like an empty shell. He didn't even know if he had gotten the words out. And before he could make up his mind to say them again, Mildred pressed a finger to his chest, right at his heart.

"Ever!" She stepped back, giving Jimmy a little breathing room. "Pull a stunt like that again—" her voice hit the words like a hammer on nails "—and it'll make your head spin how fast I can pack bags." Mildred turned and started to leave the kitchen.

Not getting a chance to say sorry, Jimmy didn't feel like trying to say it again now. He meant to speak with sarcasm, but the moment when he could have done so had passed, and the words just came out wrapped in sullenness.

"That's just great," he said to her back, which was a good deal less threatening than her front had been.

"Pack your bags and go running to mamma at the first sight of trouble. I thought you had more in you than that, Mildred."

Mildred stopped on the threshold of the living room. Jimmy thought she would turn around and say something, but she didn't. Instead, she spoke over her shoulder, almost as an afterthought, as if turning around made for more trouble than it was worth.

"I'm not talking about *my* bags."

"Let's just say," Mildred told Caleb and Joyce, "that life got cold for a few weeks before Christmas." She reached up and pulled her glasses off, rubbing her eyes like she was rubbing the image of bad things off them. "If we were having us a polite feud back that fall, what we had in December was something else." Mildred looked up at the ceiling, almost as if she were looking for the words to pull out of the air to describe it.

"Hey," Caleb put in, "why don't I go fix a little popcorn to snack on?"

"Oh, that's all right," Mildred said. "Don't reckon I need any."

"He wasn't really asking if *we* wanted any," Joyce said. "He's gotten where he snacks on popcorn about every night. What he's *really* saying," Joyce grinned, "is that he's willing to share *his* popcorn, and he wants you to hold the story until he gets back in here."

"Well, okay then, hotshot," Mildred said to her cousin. "Go fix some popcorn to share. It'll make the story seem more interesting anyway, when we get to that part."

"Takes a turn for the better, I hope." Caleb

disappeared into the kitchen, and Joyce and Mildred heard the sound of pots clattering together. Caleb refused to eat the microwave kind of popcorn; he liked the ritual of popping it in a pan.

Mildred picked up on Caleb's thoughts about things getting better. "Me and Jim did get back to normal, even better," Mildred told Joyce over the racket of Caleb shaking the pot back and forth across the eye of the stove. "Still, we had us a spell that I don't rightly know how to describe. We only had that one big blowup, but it took us a while to find each other again after that."

"The grimmest sort of niceness fell on us," Mildred said, thinking hard how to describe that awful time in her life. "We treated each other like company or something, careful and polite. But I think it was fear made us act that way, not love. And that's why it seemed so grim, I reckon, like every day was dark and every night too long." Mildred shook her head. "Maybe that was the worst part. Everything looked more or less normal on the outside—going to church, taking care of the children— though Jim did take to sleeping on the couch. And inside I was all achy, and sometimes I'd look at Jim and think he'd gone and left his body, he was that distant." With a look of absentmindedness, Mildred wrung her hands together and looked off into space.

"I'll tell you one thing," she finally said. "My feet were sure sore from walking on eggshells."

Chapter 16

A frosty world met Jimmy's gaze as he looked out the living room window. He stretched big, trying to touch the ceiling with his fingers. But even after his stretch, his back felt stiff. Sleeping on the couch didn't suit him. Yet after such a fight as they'd had a few weeks back, it didn't seem right to sleep with Mildred. Must have seemed that way to her, too. She hadn't come hunting him the first night, or the night after that.

Well, it had worked out okay. He'd been able to get his little surprise ready without her suspecting.

He looked over at his handiwork. There it stood, his big Christmas surprise. After putting in half a day at the mill the day before, he had taken the afternoon off to run down to Canton to the Sears store to pick it up, hidden it up in the carport attic, then waked up early to put it all together.

A week ago that day, acting normal for the children's sake as he and Mildred moved warily around each other like two tired boxers unwilling to fight, he had sat down with Johnny on the couch. His little boy was looking at the Sears Christmas catalog, which had finally come the second week of November—at least two weeks later than everyone else in the country got theirs, Jimmy figured.

"Hey, cowpoke," he'd said, sitting down hard beside the little boy, "whatcha doing?"

"Looking," Johnny said, with more expression than that single word could hardly bear.

"What do you see that's good?" Jimmy asked.

"Everything!" Johnny said with relish.

"Do you have something in particular you're looking at?"

Johnny's finger pointed to the open page. Jimmy started reading the captions out loud for the little boy as his finger moved from one item to the next.

"New! Over 60-piece Cape Canaveral Rocket Set." No need to read the prices—wouldn't mean anything to the boy. Still, his own eye caught the four-seventy-nine price tag.

"And here," he continued. "New! Roy Rogers 95-piece Mineral City. That looks pretty good, don't it?" Johnny wagged his head in agreement.

"New! Walt Disney 80-piece Zorro Set." Jimmy thought about all he'd just read. "Well, reckon they all oughta be new, comin' from a catalog! You wouldn't want some old toys, would you?"

Johnny laughed out a "no." Jimmy tickled him a little just to make sure the laugh came out good.

"Here's the one *I* really like," Jimmy confided, his voice going low, as if he were telling a big secret just he and Johnny could know about. His finger ran down to the bottom of the page, to the 130-piece Fort Apache set. "Like that?" he asked.

"Yeah," Johnny answered.

"What are you going to ask Santa to get you?" Jimmy asked.

An expression of innocent greed fell over the boy's face as he looked up, his turn now to talk low, giving away his innermost secrets. "Everything!" he repeated, then grinned like a possum.

"Now, we can't do that," Jimmy replied, chuckling. "Remember what I said before. For Santa Claus to get everywhere he needs to go, there's got to be some sort of limit for each little boy and girl. Else, if everyone asked for and got everything, Santa couldn't carry it all in one night."

"Oh," Johnny said, disappointment showing on his face.

"Besides," Jimmy went on, "that much weight'd probably kill the reindeer. You don't want to be responsible for killing reindeer, do you?"

"Naw," the little boy said.

"Reckon you'll just have to make do with what toys you get. Right?"

"Right!" Johnny agreed, his eyes now caught by the turning pages. Jimmy had turned to the costume page.

"Who's that?" Johnny asked.

"Why, that's Zorro. You know Zorro." Johnny allowed as how he did. "And there's Wyatt Earp—he always gets the bad guys. And Maverick, and Superman. And look, there're some girls, too. Why, there's Annie Oakley, and that there's a ballerina. See how pretty she is. And a nurse. She takes care of you when you're sick."

"Like Mamma?" Johnny asked. His eyes darted over to his mamma, who had just come into the living room carrying Rachel. Naptime was over, and Mildred had been taking a little nap of her own. Still a little heavy with sleep, she plopped down into a chair to cuddle her little girl until they both woke up a little better.

"No, not as good as Mamma," Jimmy said, casting a sideways glance at his wife and daughter. "Nobody will ever take as good care of you as your mamma. But, when you're really sick and in the hospital, the nurse helps out."

"Oh," Johnny said. His little hand went down and flipped the page again, pointing out an item.

"You want Santa to bring you a new gun?" Jimmy asked. Johnny nodded enthusiastically. "Don't know about that," Jimmy said. "You just got a new gun for your birthday. But it was a rifle," he mused. "Think maybe you need a pistol, too?"

Johnny answered by jumping up and drawing a pretend pistol from a pretend holster like he'd seen on TV. He let out an impressive "bang, bang" and then, incongruously, fell to the ground like he'd seen his daddy do, clutching his little chest and moaning.

Jimmy laughed, pulling Johnny up and setting him on his lap. "Well, then, you'll need a holster, too. Maybe like that one." He pointed to a pistol outfit from the *Have Gun, Will Travel* series. Sleek pistols lay beside a holster that was all black except for the white imprint of a horse.

"Horsie," Johnny said, pointing.

"Yep, that's a horsie," Jimmy agreed, "but it's a special kind. It's from a game called chess, and it's called a knight."

"Not knight," Johnny argued. "Horsie."

Jimmy laughed. "Okay, it *is* a horsie," he said, unwilling to argue with his three-year-old.

Then little Johnny began flipping backward toward the front of the catalog. He stopped at a special place, and he let out a loud "Oooh!"

A big train set lay splattered across an entire page—track, a mountain, and two separate freight trains that seemed to whiz across the page. Johnny let out a big "Choo! Choo!"

"Daddy," he said, "I want that."

Jimmy and Mildred had already decided the train set was too expensive—nearly forty dollars for one gift, and one that would probably end up being wrecked at the hands of a three-year-old. Plus, where would they put it? No, in civil conversation they'd agreed the train wasn't a good idea.

"Gotta just wait and see what Santa brings," Jimmy said, trying to move off the topic. He grabbed the catalog from his boy, closed it, and bopped him gently on the head with it. That led to a wrestling match that Jimmy decided should be a draw. After rolling around on the floor for a while, Jimmy picked up his little boy, then airplaned him down to the couch.

"Let's watch us a little television," he said, turning on the set and moving back to sit with Johnny. The little boy curled up next to his daddy.

Over the noise of the television, Jimmy said to Mildred, "Good service at church today."

"Yep," Mildred agreed. Rachel wiggled, awake enough now to want to get down, so Mildred put her on the floor, and she immediately tottered over to Johnny. She pulled herself up on the couch cushion, and Johnny reached down and helped her up beside him.

"Preacher Wingate brings a good message," Jimmy went on, trying to spark a little conversation. He wanted to be able to ease into what he really wanted to say.

"Good singing today, too," Mildred said. Neither she nor her uncle Robert had sung that morning. It had all been just congregational singing.

Mildred reached over and picked up a little sewing basket that sat on the table next to her. She made herself comfortable in the old overstuffed chair—the one everyone rightly considered to be mamma's place. That's where she'd sit and hold the children or, when they weren't in her lap, she'd read or do needlework. She turned on the lamp so she could see better.

She started in on a little doily, using a gold-laced antique white thread. Johnny sat and watched her for a moment, making up out of her head a pattern that looked like a complicated spider's web. She had stitched what looked like a flower in the center, and now she was casting thread in circular patterns around it. Johnny knew it'd sit nicely somewhere in the house when she was done, or maybe she meant it as a Christmas present. Everyone appreciated Mildred's handiwork, and they always seemed glad when she remembered a birthday or came by to cheer someone up who was ailing with one of her handmade "pretties," as Jimmy called them. Jimmy thought again, for the umpteenth time that week, what a good woman Mildred was, always willing to help folks out.

Mildred started singing to herself—quietly, so as not to disturb the television watchers. Watching Jimmy and Johnny must have put her mind on the coming holiday, because she was singing the carol she'd been practicing with Robert. Jimmy listened to the chorus: "Star of wonder, star of night…"

"Hey," he interrupted her before she could go on to the second verse. "Did I tell you I had to run by Mr. Nordwall's house yesterday? I wanted to remind him of a part that needs to be ordered right away. Expensive piece. Bobby told him about it last week, but he hasn't gotten around to it yet, so I thought I'd better check."

"That so?" Mildred replied. The tone wasn't rude, not like trying to throw up a roadblock to the conversation. But it wasn't an inviting tone, either, not one that sounded like, "C'mon, let me hear what you're about to say." Still, Jimmy figured he might as well go on.

"Saw something interesting at Mr. Nordwall's," he said. He skipped a beat, waiting to see if she wanted to ask "what's that?" She said nothing, so he continued.

"He's got one of those artificial Christmas trees. Aluminum." Again, Jimmy waited for his wife to jump in with some sign that she wanted the conversation to continue. She didn't, but neither did she say to hush up, so he plowed on.

"Kind of like this," he said, picking up the Christmas catalog from his lap. He held the catalog as if showing a fine picture. Mildred looked up and gave a cursory glance. She'd seen the cover; she knew what it looked like.

A close-up of an aluminum Christmas tree covered the front, and five fancy ornaments surrounded the text box: "Sears Christmas Book 1958." The smaller print beneath the catalog's title read in capital letters: "SHOP SEARS EASY TELEPHONE WAY." Three of the five ornaments were cutaways, where the front of the ball had been removed and a little scene could be seen inside. All three had Santa motifs—Santa walking through snow, Santa in his sleigh with a reindeer, and Santa in front of a house. Jimmy really liked those ornaments. He thought he'd never seen such a nicely decorated tree before.

"Pretty," Jimmy said. "Don't you think?"

Mildred barely looked up from her crocheting. "Yes, Jimmy, it is nice. I'm sure Mr. Nordwall's tree looks especially nice, too, being as it's probably real expensive."

A hint of sarcasm nipped at the heels of Mildred's words, but not enough that Jimmy picked up on it. All he heard was "nice," and what sounded like approval to him. Of course, that's what he wanted to hear.

So he'd gone out and made arrangements for the big surprise that would come before Christmas—all the better because no one would be expecting it.

That had been a week ago—a Sunday removed—and now Jimmy was ready to show off his big surprise. He figured it'd be the sort of sign Mildred needed to show that their bad feelings could come to a stop. Like a bouquet of flowers—only bigger and shinier.

He heard some stirring from back in the bedrooms. Little Johnny, unless he was mistaken, had probably just jumped in on Mildred. He heard little cooing sounds from Rachel's room. No, it wouldn't be long until he

got to enjoy the look on the smiling faces of his family.
And with that smiling, things would start setting themselves right.

Chapter 17

Caleb came from the kitchen carrying three red plastic bowls of popcorn. After handing them out like he was the waiter at a five-star restaurant, he sat himself down.

"Are we to the tree part yet?" Caleb asked with an elaborate fake yawn. "Gotta go to bed before morning, you know."

"Caleb Smith!" Joyce reached over and play-slapped his arm. "You just sit and listen. Only thing you got to do tomorrow is whatever I tell you."

With a satisfied wink, Joyce sat back and grabbed a big handful of popcorn. Mildred held up just one kernel, looking it over carefully, like it held the key to something special. A grin finally unfolded underneath her eyes that seemed to brighten them up.

"That's all right, Joyce," she said, a little energy running through her voice. "Patience isn't Caleb's strong point. That's why he's never made up a good garden of his own his whole life."

"Hey!" Caleb interjected. But then he stopped. The garden part was right, anyway. "So, what about the tree? Where's the tree come in?"

"Well, that's just it," Mildred said. "That tree you hauled down today was supposed to be Jim's peace offering, so to speak. I just walked out one morning and there it was, all put together and about as ugly a thing as you could ever see."

"My word," Joyce said. "An aluminum Christmas tree? To make up?"

"Yep, that's what he figured. I thought it to be… well, best not to say what I thought when I saw it. Still, it helped patch things up by being there, I reckon, and even more so when it wasn't."

Caleb rolled his eyes, dramatically asking, "So there's more to the story?"

"Yep," Mildred said, crunching down hard on the popped kernel that had just been the object of her inspection.

Mildred walked into the living room cradling Rachel in one arm and holding Johnny's hand in the other. Her "bed head" made her hair look wild, and the look of a good sleep interrupted lay plastered on her face. Seeing the aluminum Christmas tree stopped her dead in her tracks. Her mouth opened, the shock of it all cutting off any words that might come out.

But excitement grabbed Johnny. "Wow!" he yelled, letting go of his mamma's hand and running to the tree. "Wow!" he yelled again as the tree changed colors. On the floor, several feet from the tree, a round plastic dish revolved—translucent, with blue, red, and green sections. Behind it, a contraption looking like a tin can held a light bulb and targeted candescence toward the disk. As the tricolored dish slowly rotated, each section moving in front of the light's path, the color of the light changed, and the aluminum tree reflected the colors.

"Wow!" Johnny said for a third time, looking up at his daddy with eyes full of wonder. "Is it ours?"

"It sure is," Jimmy replied, proud that he had impressed his boy so. "A little surprise before Christmas."

"I wanna hold the light!" Johnny said as he reached for the moving disk that just begged to be picked up.

"Unh-uh," Jimmy quickly said, taking a daddy's step over and sweeping Johnny up into the air. "Gotta leave that alone. Okay?"

Just then, Mildred asked, "What about Rachel?"

"What about her, honey?" Jimmy said, throwing in the term of endearment to cue Mildred in on how this particular gift was supposed to function—something to bridge the distance that had come up between them.

Concern crept into Jimmy's mind. Mildred's question had been a little rough in the asking, and her too-sleepy-to-get-up face had not brightened at what she saw. As a matter of fact, the corners of her open mouth now turned downward. She wore a frown that Jimmy recognized. He started talking—too fast.

"Why, what do you mean, sweetheart? What about Rachel? She's not going to bother things, is she, Johnny? You're gonna help Mamma keep Rachel away from the light—right, Johnny?"

The next thing that happened surprised Jimmy. Instead of following her frown with an explanation on why she ought to be frowning and what in the world

Jimmy was going to do about it, Mildred said quietly, so quietly that Jimmy heard the disappointment in her voice right away, "So we're not all gonna go get a tree? We've always gone out to get the Christmas tree together. Rachel's never done it."

Jimmy looked at Mildred, trying to gauge what was happening, wanting to figure out why this surprise didn't seem to be working its magic, not with Mildred, anyway. He saw a tear run down her face.

"We have us a tree," Jimmy explained. "Nobody has to fool with a tree now. I took care of it."

The nakedness of his need for approval struck Mildred. She didn't like sleeping alone; she didn't like the way she and Jimmy just tolerated each other; she didn't like the pretense of normal when nothing was normal. And she certainly didn't like that tree that stood in her living room.

She knew Jimmy was trying to do something nice. Problem was, everything she knew added up to almost nothing. She wondered what in the world had happened to her and Jimmy, so far apart now that he thought what he'd done was a favor, that he didn't know the first thing about her or what she liked. And maybe she didn't know him. Not really. Maybe the business of raising children and running the household had taken up so much of her attention that she didn't pay much mind to Jimmy.

The changing colors of the aluminum Christmas tree gave the living room an eerie glow. Where was she? Mildred wondered. Was this her house? What did she know? There stood the man she made meals for, made beds for, made love to. And for a second, all she could think was that she had no idea who he was. Something about the stress of it all, the simmering anger, frustration always on the tip of her tongue, something about trying to act in a way that wasn't her in order to get along with a husband who wasn't the man she married.

A little thing, that tree. A big thing, that tree. Everything and nothing.

The tree screamed at her: Look how little any of you know about each other!

She stood there exhausted. Every night for the past week she'd gone to bed so dog-tired she thought she'd rather be dead, just so she could get some rest. But then she lay there waiting for Jimmy, wanting him to come, figuring on ordering him away when he did, knowing him too polite now to come without an invitation, and getting angrier and angrier with him for needing one. And she thought on the little things that seemed all wrong. The weight of them drove her soul into the ground. And now came that little tree, so wrong in so many little ways.

Mildred slumped into her chair. She held Rachel tight. She tried to keep back the tears. It didn't work.

The sob echoed like a crash, a soul falling down within itself. In all his married life, Jimmy had never heard that sound, and it shook him hard because he recognized the sound of bone-deep sadness when he heard it. And it shook him hard because, despite their misunderstandings of late, he loved his wife and needed to protect his family.

As an instinctive response, he pulled Johnny up into his arms before going over to Mildred. And when he got to her, he placed Johnny in her lap, so the little boy was close to his sister, and then Jimmy wrapped his arms around the three of them.

"I can take it down," Jimmy started, baffled that his plan hadn't worked but feeling the need to make things better. "I didn't have any idea you'd hate it," he said, speaking as quickly as possible so he'd have room in his brain to think about what else he should say. But his brain felt empty, and he couldn't come up with anything soothing to say, or anything clever, or any good word that would set things all right because, frankly, he didn't know what-all was wrong. And he, just like Mildred, had had the wrongness of it all seep into him, sapping his energy, so he just couldn't think what to do anymore. So he just held tight to his little group, holding them like he was on a ship, trying to keep them from all sliding overboard.

And then he said the only other words he could, words that sounded so small in the face of the enormous, shapeless void that had risen in their lives. Words that had been said so often, so worn out, that it was a wonder anyone listened to them anymore. "I'm sorry."

At that point, Mildred really did begin to cry. She held Rachel close, and Johnny reached up and put his arms around his mamma, saying the words he had heard her say so many times. "It'll be all right, Mamma."

And after a while, it was all right.

The streams of tears watered the parched places in Mildred's soul, and she felt better.

Being who she was, she was a little ashamed for breaking down in front of her family like she had. But thoughts about that disappeared when she finally had cried her eyes out and looked into her husband's eyes.

She saw there a man ashamed of himself. And not just a little. She saw in him a pain that ran deep, a pain she hadn't really noticed so much before. And for some reason, at some level, Mildred came to understand that, even though Jimmy really was sorry for how the tree had made her feel, what she was seeing in him now was really a sorrow for being who he was. He literally was ashamed of himself, and it had nothing to do with the tree.

Because of that—or maybe because it just seemed to be the right thing to say—Mildred said in a tear-stained voice, "I love you, Jimmy Jackson. These children love you. Don't you forget that—ever." And then she buried her head in his chest, and she left it there for the short while it took for the children to start squirming. Sensing the crisis was over, Johnny expressed a healthy interest in breakfast, and so the demands of a three-year-old's stomach got the family up and moving again.

They ate breakfast and cleaned up. Then they dressed for church. And they talked about the tree some. Jimmy kept insisting it would be no trouble to take it down. Mildred, her good sense asserting itself, decided that would be silly, since the thing was already bought and put up. Might as well have it up for this one Christmas, anyway. She admitted that Johnny especially seemed to like the lights. She knew Jimmy had been trying to be nice, and she told him so, and she told him she really appreciated him working to patch things up between them. She gave him a little kiss and made the point that they'd make up proper when he took back his sleeping place that night.

And then for a short while, the little period of time

when neither Johnny nor Rachel called for attention, it was like courting days again, the days when they'd simply get lost in the sound of each other's voices, taking slow walks to nowhere just to spend time in each other's company. And so Mildred talked, and Jimmy, once he had gotten into his Sunday best, sat on the bed and listened as she finished putting herself together for church.

What they talked about was Christmas when they were little.

Mildred told him about how much fun she'd always had with Christmas trees when she was little. There had been one special year, she said, right before her granny died, when she and Uncle Robert and cousin Caleb had gone out to find the perfect tree for Granny's house, looking first at one, then at another. And she and Caleb had gone out and gathered up all the rocks needed to hold the tree up in the bucket it was set in. They'd made a great game of it; called it hunting for Christmas rocks. To cap it all off, they'd gotten to pop popcorn, string it and eat it both, so that the decorations tasted as good as they looked.

As he listened, Jimmy realized that going and getting the tree and putting it up reminded Mildred about when she was little, reminded her of good times and family love. And it struck him as odd that he'd never realized that before. After all, he'd always had a tree in his house at Christmas, too, when he was growing up. But his daddy had pretty much just dragged along the first tree he saw, and he had never asked Jimmy or any of the other children to help. His mamma had been in charge of decorations, and all Jimmy remembered about that was being told to get out of the way and let her do what needed to be done.

So getting the tree wasn't anything special to him. It was just something that needed to happen for Christmas to come. And truth be told, before he married and had a family of his own, Christmas had always gone better in the dreaming than it had in reality. The people in the Sears catalog looked a whole lot happier about Christmas than anyone around his house had ever been. He and his brothers always got a little something, which of course he liked. But deep down inside, he'd always hungered for something more. Sitting there on the bed and listening to Mildred, he realized he had it now. He didn't have to keep looking in the catalog for it.

Finally, they were ready to head for church. As they went out the door, any number of things running through Jimmy's head, he let out with the first thought that slowed down enough for him to catch it in words.

"Was it big?" he asked Mildred.

"What's that, honey?" she said.

"That special Christmas tree of yours, back when you was little. Do you remember it being like the biggest, best tree you ever had?"

Mildred turned her head a little, almost as if she were listening to someone. And then the prettiest smile Jimmy had seen in a long time graced Mildred's face. "Didn't matter whether it was big or little," she stated matter-of-factly. "Love makes everything bigger. We always had a big tree, whether it stood tall or not."

Chapter 18

All the way to church, Jimmy thought on what Mildred had said—inasmuch as he could hear himself think at all. Releasing the tension that had been simmering in the house had been like popping a cork on a bottle. Johnny and Rachel both seemed to be bubbling over, and the racket they made normally would have brought a "hush a little" from Mamma or Daddy. But on that day, on that particular drive to church, there was no hushing.

They had taken the Sunliner to church. There was no question of putting the top down, it being mid-December. In fact, Jimmy hadn't really had much chance to drive with the top down at all. But he took a lot of pride in how shiny he kept her, and he counted the good feeling of driving that beautiful car a kind of compensation for all the mess he had to face at work these days.

They pulled up about the same time the crowd from Ellijay got there—Mildred's mother and father and her uncle Robert. Everyone unloaded at about the same time.

And the first words out of Lois's mouth were predictable: "Guess you figured to show off the new car, eh?"

That ate at Jimmy. The way the morning had worked out, he was in no mood to really have words with his mother-in-law, but he couldn't let her comment pass unanswered. So, in as friendly a way as he could, he said, "I work hard for what I got."

"Sure you do," Lois agreed, though the tone in her voice didn't sound agreeable. "Course," she added, looking back at the convertible then to Jimmy, "lots of folks work hard for what they don't have."

Sounded like a challenge, right there in the church parking lot.

"I hear things, you know," Lois continued as they all ambled toward the church doors. No one really wanted to stand around outside in the cool damp December air, so there wasn't the usual crowd of people you'd see milling around before church in warmer weather. "Reckon down at work, some folk figure you to be—"

Before Lois got out another word, Mildred put Johnny's hand in Jimmy's, adjusted the way she carried Rachel, and took a quick step in front of her mother.

"Stop," she said.

"Stop what?" Lois asked, looking at Mildred like she'd gone mad.

"Stop talking to Jimmy that way," she said. "We all know things stand kinda tense at work. And maybe the way you'd handle it ain't the way I'd handle it." Mildred raised her eyebrow ever so slightly, doing her best to look her mamma straight in the eye. "He does his best. He does what he thinks is right. You can't ask anything else of a man. So let him be."

Mildred had never talked that way to her mother. Surprise jumped from Lois's eyes, and something else, too. Her head nodded just a tiny bit, as if confirming something to herself. And it was with a good deal less heat than folks might have expected that she said, "Well, land sakes, child, I ain't talking to Jimmy in any sort of way, 'cept to be talking. Don't go making something out of nothing."

No one quite knew how to take that little speech until Lois said, "Gimme that baby to carry. She ain't seen her granny all week." So Lois took Rachel off Mildred's hands and walked proudly up the church steps as if she were leading them all off to the promised land.

Henry trotted up to grab the door. Mildred slipped back and slid her arm into Jimmy's, giving him a shy smile. Her uncle Robert came up from behind and patted her shoulder. As she turned to look at him, he have her a big wink and laughed, like he'd just beheld the dangdest thing he'd ever seen.

"Anyway," Mildred said, pushing the popcorn around in her bowl until she found a piece that suited her, "I figured since me and Jim had made up, last thing we needed was Mamma setting folks all on edge again. What we needed was a little peace and quiet. So I tried to make sure we got it."

She paused while she bit down on the kernel she'd chosen. "Wasn't just that me and Jim had a good talk as a result of that aluminum Christmas tree. There was something more to it than that. I think church that morning had something to do with it, though I'm not sure what. But from that point on, things went from good to better."

A satisfied look fell on her face. "Figure the Lord does work in mysterious ways," she said. "I think Him and Jim had a talk that morning, but I never reckoned it polite to barge in on others' conversations unless invited."

Mildred had to give Caleb "the look" as a guffaw he meant to suppress came out, along with a couple of half-chewed pieces of popcorn.

Church was good that day. Everyone expected to warm the place up with lively singing, and that's what they did. Preacher Wingate prayed beautifully—almost poetry, the way he sounded. And a quartet had come to sing from over Gates Chapel way.

Mildred noticed that Jimmy paid attention to everything that went on. He sang with gusto, which most people counted about as good as singing on pitch. He even amened several of Preacher's prayer petitions. But the quartet seemed to hold something special for him, and Mildred noticed that he leaned forward, soaking up the music and the message.

They did an outstanding job singing a couple of Christmas carols, even though Christmas wouldn't come until Friday. Of course, they sang some standards, too, and the tenor had the type of high voice that Mildred thought lent such a heavenly quality to gospel singing. She hummed along as the quartet sang,

Jesus is tenderly calling thee home—
Calling today, calling today....

On the second verse, she felt Jimmy shift in his seat.
She looked over and saw a man caught up in listening.

Jesus is calling the weary to rest—
Calling today, calling today;
Bring him thy burden and thou shalt be blest;
He will not turn thee away.

By the third verse, she heard him heave out a breath
of sorrow, saw his shoulders sag, and beheld a man
bone-tired with a weariness sleep alone couldn't cure.
She knew something was going on with him, but she
didn't know exactly what it was, so she just kept her
attention tuned to him while Preacher Wingate walked
up to give the sermon.

It was a good one—even with her attention distracted,
Mildred knew that. Preacher started in talking about how
Christmas was coming up and reminding the people
about the shepherds who were first to hear about the
coming of Jesus. And then he reminded them that Jesus
Himself claimed to be the good shepherd—talked about
the sheep recognizing His voice, and how He knew all
His sheep.

"Knows us all!" he said, slapping the pulpit for
emphasis. "He's the good shepherd. He's my shepherd.
He knows me by name. He calls out to me. And if I'll
listen, I'll hear His voice."

He took a deep drink of water from the glass that
somebody always filled before church. "He knows you,
too. Knows you top to bottom. Knows how many hairs
are on your head. Knows every thought you ever had."

Preacher rapped his skull so loudly Mildred heard it. She imagined it might have hurt. But Preacher went on.

"Most important," he said, "most important, He knows what's in here." He pointed to his heart, his hand over it like he was saying the pledge of allegiance. "He knows you because He knows what's in your heart. And so, knowing everything there is to know about you, He calls you by name. Telling you to come. 'Come and be with Me,' He says. 'Come and rest your weary bones. Come and lay down all your cares.' "

He wiped his brow with a handkerchief. "What'd the singers say? 'Jesus is calling the weary to rest.' You hear what else they sung? They said Jesus is pleading—the Son of God Almighty, Jesus Christ the light of the world Himself, is pleading. 'Hear Him,' the song says. And I'll say it, too: Hear Him. Hear Him call your name. Hear Him. He knows you. He knows who you are. He won't turn you away. Just come. Come to Jesus."

And with that, Preacher Wingate finished.

The music for the final hymn started. The piano called the congregation to join in. Preacher chose just the right song to end the service, one to go with the fine quartet music that had accompanied the sermon in such a fitting fashion. After the usual playing through of the first verse, the congregation started in on "Softly and tenderly Jesus is calling…" And by the time they hit the chorus, Mildred noticed that Jimmy had the wiggles.

Come home, come home,
Ye who are weary, come home;
Earnestly, tenderly, Jesus is calling,
Calling, O sinner, come home!

Something like a silent struggle transpired during that hymn. As usual, little Johnny did his best to hold the hymnbook for his mamma so she could sing and hold Rachel at the same time. Mildred rocked gently back and forth on her heels, swaying to the music. But out of the corner of her eye, she kept watch on Jimmy. At the last verse, whatever had been happening inside Jimmy finished up. He walked down the aisle toward Preacher as the congregation sang.

Preacher watched as Jimmy came forward. He briefly looked at the song leader and nodded. With that, the leader knew to start back with the first verse. As long as someone stood at the altar, or kneeled, the music would continue. And that was important. It made things less awkward—the congregation had something to do while matters of sin and salvation were prayed over between Preacher and whoever stood there. It made the congregation feel like their singing supported those who walked the aisles, letting them know the voices of heaven rejoiced at the saving of a lost soul. But the music kept up for another reason, too. It blanketed Preacher and the soul searcher in privacy, the quiet words of spiritual battle kept between the altar participants.

Jimmy finally stopped in front of Preacher. As was his wont, Preacher held out his hand to Jimmy, and when Jimmy responded, Preacher placed his other hand on top of that, holding on, giving assurance. He waited for Jimmy's eyes to meet his. "What can Jesus do for you today, Jimmy? All you gotta do is ask."

Preacher Wingate, by all accounts, was pretty good in the pulpit. But more than the average run of country preachers, he listened well. And he had a sensitive streak in him that lots of times made other folks' troubles apparent to him—not the exact problems, but the fact that they were struggling somewhere deep inside. All this meant that, once he opened up a door for talking, he knew enough to shut his own mouth. He stood eager to help, to pray, to speak words of assurance and salvation. But he never spoke them too soon; he waited. And that was a good thing, because it took Jimmy a little while to get started that morning.

"Preacher," Jimmy whispered, words barely audible over the sea of song in which he and Preacher stood awash, "does Jesus really know who I am? Does He know me?"

Preacher took more than a second to respond to Jimmy's need. "Jesus knows exactly who you are, what you have been, what you can be." He paused, let that sink in, and added, "By name, by heart. Jesus knows you, Jimmy."

Then Jimmy's gaze took on a yearning air, a begging quality that his voice, in its trembling, worked hard to mask.

"Will He tell me?"

"Tell you what, Jimmy?"

"Who I am. Who I'm supposed to be. Do you believe Jesus will tell me that?"

Preacher took a long time answering. His chin hit his chest as he closed his eyes, listening for a voice that would guide him in his guiding.

"If you listen," Preacher finally said, looking up, coming out of himself to meet Jimmy's searching eyes, "if you listen hard, I do believe that, Jimmy. Jesus will tell you who you are, what He sees, what you can be. But you have to listen."

"How?" Jimmy asked.

"Just pay attention. Jesus comes to us in all sorts of ways. Some see Him in a trout stream, others in their neighbor. At work, in the fields. Anywhere. Everywhere." Preacher smiled a self-deprecating smile. "Even in church, people see Jesus, and if they listen, they hear Him. You can, too, Jimmy. Look for Him. Read your Bible. Listen. I think He'll tell you what you need to know."

They knelt down together, and Preacher prayed for Jimmy, asking Jesus to open his eyes, his ears, his heart. And when they were through praying, Jimmy made his way back to Mildred and his children, his in-laws and his friends. Since it wasn't exactly a saving, there'd be no standing in the back shaking hands with everyone as they filed out. So they finished up the verse they were on, Preacher prayed a short prayer for dismissal, and church ended.

Slowly the church emptied, voices talking about how good church had been, or what sat in the cook pots at home, or what the week's weather might bring, or whose family was visiting for Christmas.

No one said anything to Jimmy about going up front. Church etiquette held that altar talks remained private unless the one who walked forward indicated that he wanted to say something about it all. Jimmy didn't, so everyone respected his privacy.

After a little milling around—not much because of the nippy weather—Mildred and Jimmy, each with a child in their arms, headed off to the car. They had already said their goodbyes to Lois, Henry, and Robert, but not long ones—they'd be meeting up again later for Sunday dinner. Then they heard a familiar clank and shuffle, and they turned around and saw Bobby Ferguson coming at them.

"Hey, Jacksons," he said, flashing a mouthful of teeth at them like they were the best thing he'd seen in ages.

"Well hey, Bobby," Mildred said, just as Jimmy had given his own salutation. "Good to see you."

"And you're just the purdiest little family I ever seen," Bobby shot back.

"Who's with Paul?" she asked, knowing Bobby never left his brother alone for more than a few minutes. Paul was Bobby's older brother, but he hadn't been right since he came home from the big war in Europe. He couldn't be trusted not to wander away.

"Oh, got family visiting from over Turniptown way," he replied. "They came last night, and we had such a good time they figured they'd just stay on a spell. Daddy's brother and wife. Told 'em I'd like to get to church, so they're sitting with Paul."

"Got plans for Christmas?" Jimmy asked, wondering if Bobby'd have family over or if he'd be taking Paul off somewhere.

"Naw, not really," Bobby replied. "We're heading off on Christmas Eve for a little while. Mamma's side of the family's having a little get-together 'round suppertime after everybody gets off work. But it'll just be me and Paul on Christmas day. Miss Stover's taking off to visit some kin down in Calhoun."

"She's so nice," Mildred said with emphasis. Miss Stover had taught all of them at Harmony School, the same school where Mildred had taught for a while. Long retired from teaching, she watched Paul during the work-week and helped Bobby with the housekeeping.

"Yep. Don't rightly know what I'd do without her," Bobby allowed. "But I'm glad she's getting a little time to herself." Then he got to the point of his little visit.

"Said you had some car work you wanted done, Jimmy?"

"Oh, that's right," Jimmy responded. "Mildred's car is knocking. Do you have time to work on it before Christmas?"

Bobby thought a second. "If you don't mind leav-ing it for a couple of days. Can't work on it during the day, course, but I can look it over after I get home from work." Bobby figured in his head a second, making sure he could do what he was about to promise. "Drop it by the house tomorrow night, and I'll have it ready to go 'fore lights out on Wednesday. That way, it'll be ready to drive up to the North Pole on Thursday, grab those toys 'fore Santa gets 'em on the sleigh, and be home for Christmas dinner on Friday." Bobby aimed those last words at Johnny. "Or reckon you can count on ol' Santa Claus to bring your toys?"

Not much of what Bobby said had made the least impression on Johnny, but the little boy's ears pricked up when he heard about Santa Claus coming with toys. He squirmed a little in his daddy's arms, buried his head in his daddy's shoulder, then looked back with an impish grin and said simply, with all the delight one word could hold, "Santa!"

Then everybody heard Mildred let off a little "ooh!"

"What's the matter, honey?" Jimmy asked.

"Just got hit by a big raindrop, right on the nose." She reached up to wipe it away, and they all looked up at the sky. It'd been a gray day to start with, and there were still plenty of clouds. But there had been a little break, and the sun was shining through, so it surprised them all just a little bit when several large drops started to splatter around them. It was like a little warning shot, a message that, despite the sunshine, they'd better take cover.

Little Johnny looked up at the sky in amazement, seeing the sunshine, feeling a drop of rain here and there, looking like it was the biggest puzzle he'd ever seen.

"Devil's beating his wife," Bobby said.

"Huh?" Johnny looked confused.

"My goodness," Bobby said, looking at Jimmy and Mildred. "Ain't you never taught your son nothing?" They just laughed.

Bobby looked at the little boy and said, "When it's sunshiny and raining at the same time, that means the devil's beating his wife." And with that bit of folk wisdom, Bobby turned around and made for his car in earnest. He didn't figure on getting soaked, no matter how the devil treated his wife.

Chapter 19

"So," Mildred said, getting near the end of her popcorn, picking up each piece like it was precious, "those few days right after Sunday were awful nice. And Christmas, that was about the most special Christmas I ever had." Memories of goodness seemed to march across Mildred's face. "A good time, that," she said, and Joyce and Caleb both nodded their heads, enjoying her enjoyment.

"Except for that little unpleasantness when Jim got fired," she added.

"Oh," Caleb said with a smirk, "except for that one little thing."

"Well, it turned out to be the best thing ever happened to Jim," Mildred said, saying it like she meant it as much as she'd ever meant anything in her life.

"Pop, I can handle it," Claude Nordwall told his father.

"How? How, son? How does this possibly work out?"

Old man Nordwall spoke in an especially belligerent tone. "Maybe your brother can straighten things out. I'll call him."

"No!" It was Mr. Nordwall's turn to fume. "We're practically there right now. Just gotta tweak the production schedule a little."

"Don't try to fool me," the old man said, sounding madder now. "I can read figures. I can listen to reports." Age and bourbon gave his voice an edge, made him sound horribly old.

"I can…"

"You can't do anything," the old man cut in. "But I'll give you one more chance. Now really, how far behind are you?"

Mr. Nordwall bristled at the notion that any of this was his fault. "Not more than a day, and we'd be completely caught up."

"It's a day we don't have. I promised shipment in time for installation after Christmas. You got that? That means that they have to have the entire order the day after Christmas."

"Pop, they can't possibly mean that. If they have the lion's share of it, what does it matter if a little comes in late? They can't possibly have the people to get it all in by the first of the year."

"I don't care," the old man emphasized. "I said they'd have the shipment, complete, no later than the day after Christmas."

"But if we pull a shift on Saturday—"

"Then they don't get it until Sunday. And it throws the trucking schedule off. And they have to be able to run it through the inventory process. We get that carpet to them on Sunday, they don't start laying it until Tuesday at earliest. Too late. First of the year's on that Friday. They need to have it in-house by Saturday in order to be ready to run with it on Monday. Monday, son. You know your days of the week, don't you?"

Mr. Nordwall thought his head would blow clean off his shoulders. "Pop, don't talk to me like that."

"Like what, son?" the old man asked. "Like a businessman getting ready to fire someone who apparently can't do his job?"

"Pop," Mr. Nordwall said, trying his best to control his anger and his fear and his insecurities and his past— all of which, if it had come out, would have been one long scream. "I'll have it loaded and ready to ship by Saturday morning."

"How, son, how?"

"I'll pull together a crew to work Christmas Day," Mr. Nordwall said, knowing that that's what his father had wanted to hear since the conversation had started.

"And son," the old man said, "get that supervisor of yours to take the heat for it." Then there was a click.

Mr. Nordwall slammed the receiver down, the scream still tickling the back of his throat.

If his secretary hadn't been right outside his door, he wouldn't have bothered to hold it in.

Jimmy and Mildred walked slowly to the Sunliner from the Holt's house.

"Fine chicken," Jimmy said, running a toothpick along his front teeth. At times he had doubts about Lois's being the best mother-in-law possible, but he had no such doubts about her cooking. "Nice to have such a meal in the middle of the day."

Mildred playfully poked him in the side. "Nice to have such company in the middle of the day on a Wednesday. Wish my car was broken more often."

"Well, Bobby'll have that taken care of by tonight," Jimmy said, putting his arm around Mildred and pulling her close. "Still, it's nice to have a driver for the day." Mildred smiled.

"I'll have the shopping done by quitting time," she said, "then I'll swing by and pick you up. We'll get the children last. Mamma likes having all the time she can get with them."

"Sounds good to me," Jimmy said. He looked at his watch. "Oh, we'd better get going—too much to do, too little time to do it, and me five minutes late." Mildred could tell by the sound of his voice that, inside his head, he'd already switched to work mode.

They pulled into the mill lot, parking in Jimmy's special supervisor's spot. Though he knew he was running late, he didn't act as if he wanted their little middle-of-the-day date to end.

"Why don't you come in with me," he suggested. "See me to my desk, say hello to Bobby. Generally make everybody in the whole mill jealous that I've got the prettiest wife in all of Gilmer County."

Mildred swung her legs out of the car. No way a girl could turn down an invitation like that.

They walked down the hallway toward Jimmy's office. But as they got there, they heard commotion down the hall in the factory area, so they went to see what was going on.

All the workers had gathered to listen to Mr. Nordwall. He stood on an upside-down crate, glaring down at the workers as if he found them repulsive, as if he wanted to turn and run. Then he saw Jimmy, and relief popped up on his face—relief and something else. He'd had a nasty surprise when he had his secretary call everyone together and then discovered that Jackson wasn't back from lunch yet. This would make up for it.

"Well, Mr. Jackson," Nordwall said, "glad you could join us." With special emphasis, he added, "Hope you had a nice meal. Good to have a company car to get you where you want to go, here in the middle of the day."

Jimmy stiffened, and Mildred stopped in her tracks. They both sensed something wrong in the air, but they didn't know what. Mildred thought Nordwall looked like a crazy man, a wild sort of grin appearing on his face.

"I have an important announcement to make." Mr. Nordwall gathered himself up, trying to look big. Mildred wondered if he would go so far as to stand on tiptoe.

"Not everyone has done their job." People moaned. Mr. Nordwall put out his hand, calling for silence. "We're behind in our production schedule. But I can't say that it's your fault—you couldn't have known. The plant supervisor oversees production, and Mr. Jackson should have kept on top of things."

This time wind escaped between Jimmy's teeth in a low whistle. Mildred tightened her hold on Jimmy's arm.

"Any rate, this operation has made commitments, all

of which it intends to keep," Nordwall declared. "We are behind on those commitments, but we *will* honor them. Therefore…" He paused. He took in a deep breath. "Therefore," he repeated, "we will have to run a full shift on Christmas Day."

At this point, a great deal of mumbling broke out.

"Not all of you," Nordwall went on, "just half of you. We've got to pull one full shift on Christmas Day. Half of you, half of second shift. And of course," Mr. Nordwall said, a look of maniacal glee in his eyes, "since Mr. Jackson, in his capacity as plant supervisor, is responsible for meeting the production schedule, he will spend the next few minutes deciding which of you will work. Right, Mr. Jackson?"

With that, Nordwall started to make his way to the office, coming to the place where Mildred and Jimmy stood at the entrance to the office hallway.

"Wait a minute," someone said. It was Bobby. Almost as if being pulled against his will, Nordwall slowed down, then turned around.

Bobby made his way through the crowd. The clanking of his brace echoed throughout the work area. He finally made it to where Nordwall was, which was close to where Mildred and Jimmy stood. He nodded his head at Mildred, then turned to Mr. Nordwall.

"Mr. Nordwall, I told you a coupla weeks ago that the matting rig needed a new part. You told me just to keep the thing running, which is what I've done. Did you ever order the part?" Bobby's eyes burned into Nordwall, a special urgency in the question.

For the briefest second confusion crossed Mr.

Nordwall's face. Then he straightened and looked at Bobby with a look that said he couldn't be bothered. "No, I never got around to it—which is why you have to be one of the Christmas Day Santas. Carpet presents for everyone." With that, Mr. Nordwall turned to leave.

"Naw, don't reckon I will." The voice wasn't loud, but there was no mistaking its seriousness.

Mr. Nordwall wheeled around. "I reckon," Mr. Nordwall said, mimicking the mountain accent, "you will."

"Naw," Bobby said. "Can't do it. Me and my brother are having Christmas together, just him and me."

"Well, go tell your brother," Mr. Nordwall said, his voice pitching higher, "that he'll be spending Christmas by himself, because you're going to be here, or else you'll have no job." He turned on his heel again.

A voice rang out clear. "That's not right. Bobby's brother can't be by himself." The voice belonged to Mildred.

Mr. Nordwall sucked in his breath, then turned on the source of challenge to his authority. By now, his face shone red.

"Jackson," he barked out, "don't you know how to keep your wife in line?" He gave Jimmy the up and down, then addressed Mildred. "Why are you in my plant? You have no job here. You have no business here. And if you don't leave, I'll have you thrown out." Then almost as an aside, he mumbled, "Stupid woman."

Surprise, then anger, swept across Mildred's face. Jimmy stood there, mouth slightly ajar. She looked at him to see what he would do, but he seemed frozen. Nordwall spoke acid when he turned to Jimmy again. "If you don't get her out of here, you'll have no company car, no Christmas bonus, and no job."

That took some of the wind out of what Mildred was about to say. No car she could live with. But Jimmy needed his job, and they needed the bonus he'd been promised for meeting the Christmas season production quotas. Two weeks' salary would go a long way to paying off what they owed Sears. So, instead of saying anything, she just stood there, not knowing what to do.

A clanking noise rang out as Bobby positioned himself between Mildred and Mr. Nordwall. The boss looked confused again, like he wasn't sure where the other man had come from.

"Listen good," Bobby said, words slicing the air between himself and Nordwall. "One, if you try to make me work Christmas Day, I'll quit. That simple. Two," he added, and Mildred saw his fists clinch. "You'll make proper apologies to Mrs. Jackson for the way you just talked to her. And if you don't," he said, stretching out his arm and pointing a finger at Nordwall, "I'll beat it out of you. That is a promise."

A collective gasp came from the mill hands. They knew Bobby. If he said he'd do something, he would.

Mr. Nordwall's breath came hard. Instinctively, he looked around for help. He saw none. All eyes were on him and Bobby—all eyes except Mildred's. She looked at Jimmy again. She saw a struggle pass across his countenance, but only briefly. Then she noticed how he turned his head, just a little bit, the kind of turn you see on people when they've had their name called and they don't know where the voice came from. Then she saw something that made her heart smile. She saw his eyes.

It's said you can see it in a man's eyes when he snaps. It was like that for Jimmy, but in a good way. He saw Bobby standing between Mr. Nordwall and Mildred, and it was like something snapped together for him rather than apart. You could see the click in his eyes almost as clearly as you can hear the click of a shotgun when it's loaded and snapped shut.

He stepped forward, placing a hand on Bobby's shoulder. His posture radiated steady ease, the kind of natural stance he'd take back in the days when he was a football star. Though easy of stance, he aimed steely eyes at Mr. Nordwall, full of the type of concentration he'd put into kicking the football, doing it better than anyone around the whole state had ever seen. And though he sounded dead serious, something like joy resonated in his voice. He said simply, "I beg your pardon, Mr. Nordwall. That's my wife you're talking to. You *will* apologize." At the same time, Jimmy and Bobby stepped toward Mr. Nordwall.

A thin lining of sweat had enveloped Mr. Nordwall's face. Fear and shock and incomprehension glistened on his face. He had no doubt that either of the two people standing in front of him could kill him, but surely they wouldn't. Would they? And wasn't he the boss? How could they talk to him this way, in his mill? And how did he lose control of this situation?

Pop will kill me for this. What to do?

Through thin lips and in an even thinner voice, Mr.

Nordwall announced, somewhat in Mildred's direction, "I'm sorry I snapped at you. Worried about business, you know. Makes a person jumpy." He thought that'd save his skin. No one was hitting him. That gave him the moment he needed to think about what to do next.

"Everyone back to work," he announced. "That is, if you want to keep your jobs." By the time he had stood there for a few moments, hands on his hips, most of them finally turned and shuffled off back to their stations, murmuring, "What about Christmas?"

That gave Mr. Nordwall the incentive to try to contain the breach in decorum and gather back his broken dignity. He glared at Bobby and Jimmy.

"You're both fired. Please leave now or I'll call the police." It didn't matter about the production schedule. There was no meeting it without Bobby and Jimmy, and he knew he couldn't count on either.

He thought he'd get the satisfaction of some sort of protest. But what he saw in Bobby looked like nothing other than complete disregard for what had been said. And Jackson looked for all the world like he had just been relieved of some burden.

Both turned immediately, Mildred between, and started walking off without so much as a goodbye. That simply wouldn't do.

"Jackson," Nordwall said, trying to bark the name out, but without any heart in it. "Forgetting something?"

Jimmy stopped and turned around. His only response a raised eyebrow.

"The car." Mr. Nordwall held out his hand. "It's not your car!"

Jimmy didn't react right away. Then Nordwall demanded, "The keys. Or full payment," he added with a sneer, knowing full well that Jimmy couldn't pay cash for the car. "The keys. You don't work here. Drive away and I'll report that car stolen."

For the first time, Jimmy realized the foolishness of the whole company car deal. A corner of his mind even admitted that his mother-in-law had been right about the arrangement. The way it had been set up didn't make a lot of sense.

"Guess you'll need a ride home," Bobby offered.

Jimmy tossed his car key to Mr. Nordwall, then he turned to walk out of a place and a job that he now knew had been wrong for him all along. Despite his trying to do right, everything had ended up wrong. More than that, he had ended up being the kind of person he didn't want to be.

"If you don't mind," he said, turning to Bobby. "I'll take you up on that offer of a ride. Got my girl here to get home." He put his arm around Mildred and gave her a light squeeze, all the more intimate because of its light touch.

"Well," Mildred put in, "at least get us to Mamma's. Got the children to pick up. Someone there can run us home later, maybe after supper."

"Have 'em run you by my place first," Bobby said. "Looks like I've got the afternoon off, so I can have your car all ready to go." He then gave a possum's grin to Jimmy. "Nordwall don't own that one, does he?"

"No, he doesn't." Jimmy grinned back, finding himself full of pride for some reason, like it was the best thing in the world not to have the mill have control of his car.

His car. His and Mildred's. And he must have realized, deep inside, that there were many things that belonged to Mildred and him that no one could touch, not if he took care of her like he should.

He knew she'd take care of him.

Chapter 20

The biggest surprise for Jimmy that day, the day before Christmas Eve, was his mother-in-law. When they got to Lois's, Mildred indicated that there was something she needed to tell her. Lois said she had a little something to tell Mildred, too, but that it was just a little something and could wait.

So Mildred explained about everything that had happened at the mill. Jimmy noticed with amazement that Lois didn't interrupt once—just sat there listening, an ability Jimmy didn't even know she had.

After Mildred finished her recitation of events, Lois looked up at the ceiling, almost as if looking to heaven for strength. Then she slowly stood up and walked over to the both of them. She stretched out her hand to Jimmy's face.

For a long time after that, Jimmy would remember the shame of that moment. For one thing, he flinched. He shouldn't have flinched in the face of a slap from a woman, even if that woman was Lois. But the real embarrassment came because he really did think that Lois was reaching out to slap him. He assumed that instead of giving him a piece of her mind, she'd be giving him the back of her hand for ruining her daughter's life, not having a job with the children to raise, and Christmas come on top of that. But what Lois actually did was lay her hand on the side of Jimmy's face and give him an affectionate pat. Then she said words that about bowled him over. "Always knew, deep down, you to be a right decent feller, Jimmy."

She turned and went back to her chair. "Do what you gotta do to make sure you take care of your family. But more'n that, be who you gotta be, and that's what'll really take care of your family."

At that moment, Lois turned a smile on Jimmy, and it shocked him because he recognized that smile—it was Mildred's. And from that day on, Jimmy knew there to be more to Lois than he had ever thought, and he was glad to know it.

"Now," Lois said, "I reckon the little bit of news I've got for you might catch your attention, knowing what I know now." She cleared her throat. Lois loved having important information to share, and she was milking it for all it was worth.

"Had a visit from Andrew Davis today." At that, Mildred's eyes widened. Mr. Davis was a local surveyor, but he also sat as chair of the Ellijay school board.

"What'd he want?" Mildred asked in anticipation.

"Oh, he's doing a little surveying for me and your daddy, up around Mamma's place. He had a few questions about the property lines."

Lois wet her lips, giving herself time as she cast

about for words. As usual, the most direct ones came to mind.

"While he was here, he asked if you had ever thought much about going back to teaching. He's got a teacher expecting, and she figures on staying home with the baby, so she's not coming back after Christmas break. Principal's not had any luck getting anybody to take her place, so he asked Mr. Davis if he knew anybody that might be fit for the job." Lois let that settle in. Then, before Mildred could say anything, she offered, "Course, wouldn't be no trouble for me to keep the young'uns, me sitting here just a stone's throw from the school."

With that, a weight fell off Mildred and Jimmy's shoulders. Quitting his job was all well and good, but neither of them forgot for a second that they had to have some way to support themselves. And just as they started talking all at once about the possibilities, Johnny came into the living room, rubbing the afternoon sleep out of his eyes. He walked over to his mamma and fell into her open arms, taking the waking up time to snuggle.

"I don't know how you get him to take a nap," Mildred said, eyeing her mother with respect. "I can't hardly get him to do it anymore."

"Just takes a granny's touch," Lois said, and Jimmy saw again that smile he had never noticed before. But it came easily enough, so maybe he just hadn't been paying attention.

One of the most pleasant afternoons Jimmy had ever spent at Lois's house passed too quickly, and soon Henry and Robert came home from work. They heard about the events of the day, and both men had about the same reaction as Lois. A substantial supper made its way to the table, and Lois asked Jimmy to return thanks. For the first time, he used the words often spoken among Mildred's family, for the first time having some notion of what was meant as he said:

"For mercy everlasting, O Lord, we're thankful."

Finally, with an air of amiableness that had been lacking the past few months, Mildred and Jimmy and Johnny and Rachel started home. Uncle Robert sat in the driver's seat, talking up a storm with Johnny. Mildred and Jimmy sat in back, Mildred holding Rachel, as they talked excitedly about the possibilities ahead of them.

By the time Robert dropped Jimmy off at Bobby's to pick up the car, Mildred and Jimmy had decided she could teach for a while, and Jimmy would concentrate on making something of the little orchard they'd started. He'd pick up work somewhere for the rest of the winter, then start headlong in the spring. He could even go back to logging for a while—needed to clear more land anyway if he was going to expand the orchard.

They both knew it'd be hard. They both knew it might not work. They both knew there'd be lean times ahead. But they both knew they were in it together, and that made everything all right. So it was with a genuine sense of well-being that Jimmy got out of the car, waved goodbye to the family, and went to rap on Bobby's door—lightly, because he knew loud noises bothered Paul. And as Bobby opened the door, Jimmy grabbed his hand and gave it a heartfelt shake, glad there were people like Bobby Ferguson in the world and knowing himself lucky to be counted as one of his friends.

"That was a lot to be going on right before Christmas," Caleb said. "Must have been unsettling."

"No, not really," Mildred replied, eyes dancing with memories. "We did all right by it all," she said, the understatement of it all apparent to everybody there.

"Well, here we are," Caleb said, feigning impatience, "end of the evening, end of the coffee, and no end to the story. What about that Christmas tree we found?"

"Little things," Mildred said. "It's the little things, after all, that really add up. They can tear you down if you let them, but it's also the little things that build you up. Keeping that tree was Jimmy's way of reminding himself of that, I think." She smiled, downing the last drop of coffee in her cup, taking the storyteller's prerogative to pause before the end of the story.

Christmas Eve came, and anticipation flooded the Jackson house. Johnny was old enough to be excited, and Jimmy and Mildred were young enough to share in it.

The day started with Jimmy standing up right after breakfast and announcing, "Before I do anything else today, I need to go say hey to Mamma." He didn't need to add that he was going to apologize. Mildred knew it. And she nodded her head in agreement as Jimmy stepped out into the cold December air.

He was gone longer than she expected, and he came back all red in the face, with a sniffly nose, like he'd been outside for some length of time.

"You okay?" she asked, going over and placing her hands over his. They were ice cold, so she started gently rubbing them.

"Everything's great," he said, and he pulled her to him, kissing her gently on the top of the head, then just holding her for a few minutes.

Mildred spent the afternoon mostly making pies for Christmas dinner, along with some homemade loaf bread. Jimmy played with Johnny and Rachel. And he wasn't half playing, half somewhere else, as had often been the case the last few months, his mind always worried about the mill. For that time, that afternoon, he belonged to his children, never wanting to be anywhere else, never thinking much about anything else.

But even the best of days finally comes to an end, made a little bittersweet by knowing that such a good day would have to live on just in memory. There'd be other good days, but never another one just like this one. Jimmy tried to burn the thought of that day into his mind, hoping to help his memory hold on to the important things—images and feelings of love and family.

They read the story about the birth of the baby Jesus. By the time they were done, Rachel had fallen asleep, so Mildred put her to bed. Then it came time to start getting Johnny ready for sleep. Jimmy had him curl up in his lap, and Mildred sat snuggled beside the two of them. Jimmy took out a book, and reading only from the tricolored glow of light that hit the aluminum Christmas tree, he started, "'Twas the night before Christmas, and all through the house…"

About an hour after Johnny had gone down for the night, Mildred let out a big yawn and announced, "Reckon it's bedtime for me, too. I'm worn out." She surveyed the pile of presents from Santa that they had just arranged under the tree. Jimmy placed his arm around Mildred's shoulder and squeezed.

"Why don't you run on to bed," Jimmy said. "I'll be there in a bit. Got a few things I still want to do."

Mildred, tired and happy, trotted off to bed. Thirty minutes later, Jimmy peeked in on her, making sure she was fast asleep. He pulled the door to, smiling to himself.

Mildred slept the sleep of those who work hard all day. Finally, she stirred, hearing noises. She reached over and placed a hand on Jimmy, then woke up with a bit of a start as she realized he wasn't there. She looked at her clock. Five o'clock. A crack of light outlined the bottom of the bedroom door, where it had been closed to keep out the light of whatever activity was going on elsewhere in the house. Now the noise had become an outright clanking, like someone beating the stove with a pot, but trying to do it quietly. She listened a little longer, then decided she'd better get up to see what was going on.

As she opened the door, the first thing to hit her was the smell—popcorn. She followed the scent down the hallway, and she stepped out into the living room just as Jimmy stepped from the kitchen into the same room. He held a big pot of popcorn.

"Merry Christmas, sweetheart," he said, smiling at her like it was important that he show every tooth in his head.

She stood disoriented for a moment. The Christmas presents had been moved to a corner of the living room, away from the tree. Why would Jimmy do that? And then, more than seeing a difference at first, she smelled a difference. Another scent broke through the warm popcorn smell.

Tree. It was the smell of a freshly cut tree.

Then she saw. There, where the aluminum Christmas tree had been, stood one of the prettiest little white pines she'd ever seen. It leaned a little to the left. She smiled when she realized that an old bucket full of rocks held the tree up. "Oh, Jimmy," she said.

She walked over to the tree, taking in what was, for her, the smell of love. Jimmy came and stood by her. The mingled smell of popcorn and tree took Mildred's mind to a place of Christmas past, where family and love meant everything. And somehow or another that past got led, by her sense of smell, into the present. A trickle of joy escaped from one eye, then both.

Jimmy recognized the goodness of those tears as he dabbed at the corners of her eyes. "Come sit down," he said, leading her to the couch. As she leaned in to him, he said, "If we're gonna have a real tree, figured we oughta have real decorations." He reached over to the end table, acting as if he were pulling a rabbit out of a hat, and held up needle and thread. "I thought if we worked hard, we'd have the popcorn put on before the young'uns wake up."

Mildred laughed and pulled Jimmy to her, kissing him hard, then saying, "We'd better get at it, then."

And they did.

"That's about the sweetest thing I've ever heard," Joyce said, her eyes red around the edges.

Acknowledging the power of Mildred's story, Caleb said simply, "Jim was a good man."

"Yes, he was," Mildred agreed. Then again, mostly to herself, she repeated, "Yes, he was."

She gave Caleb and Joyce the kind of smile that says "love you" louder than words. Then she put on her no-nonsense air and got up. "Better take this old lady home,

Caleb. Past my bedtime, and we still have lots of packing to do tomorrow. Gotta get an early start."

With only a little good-natured grumbling, Caleb raised himself out of his easy chair. Joyce watched the two cousins head out the door, each carrying a Sears catalog. She got up and began collecting coffee cups and dessert plates, humming "Amazing Grace" while she did so. Then, after washing up and putting everything away, she went and stood by the living room window, waiting for her husband to come home.

Acknowledgments

Once again, I am very happy for this opportunity to thank Rutledge Hill Press for their support. Though I owe the whole staff my gratitude, I am especially eager to acknowledge Larry Stone, who, in his role as publisher, agreed to take on this novel, and Jennifer Greenstein, whose work as editor has always inspired confidence.

I received wonderful assistance from Anne Christian Buchanan, who kept pushing me to produce a better book. Though I have not always followed her advice (authors can be stubborn), I have done so often enough that even I can tell the result is superior to what I had at first written.

A number of books were helpful as I wrote this one: *Mountain Spirits: A Chronicle of Corn Whiskey from King James' Ulster Plantation to America's Appalachians and the Moonshine Life* by Joseph Earl Dabney (New York: Scribner, 1974); *Carpet Capital: The Rise of a New South Industry* by Randall L. Patton (Athens:

University of Georgia Press, 1999); *Shaping an American Institution: Robert E. Wood and Sears, Roebuck* by James C. Worthy (Urbana: University of Illinois Press, 1984); and *Sears, Roebuck, U.S.A.: The Great American Catalog Store and How It Grew* by Gordon Lee Weil (Briarcliff Manor, N.Y.: Stein and Day, 1977). Though *The Aluminum Christmas Tree* is set primarily in 1958, the images described from the Sears catalogs (fall and Christmas) come from both 1958 and 1959.

The community of Smoky Hollow is fictional, but the town of Ellijay and the county of Gilmer in north Georgia are not. The feel of the book comes, in part, from my own experience and from the memories of my parents, Paul and Christine Davis. For this feeling of place, plus the love that makes it so powerful and positive, I thank them, along with the whole crew who still lives there: sister Denise; brother Tim and his wife, Connie; and the gang of nieces and nephews—Jason (and his wife, Gena), Christopher, Thomas, Anna, Tanner, and Ally (maybe not quite such a "gang," but it seems that way when we are together). All these people create a special place, and my daughters, Mave and Gwynne (who continue to create in me unspeakable joy), love the sense of home that emanates from this north Georgia family.

Of course, the great thing about families is that they can grow, and they do not all have to be connected to the same place. And so I want to remember others who help create in me a sense of home: Kelly and Ade; John and Aaron; Chuck and Carolyn; Michelle, Benjie, and Abbey; Trudy and Mike; and Sarah and Phil. There's more: visits with my wife's parents and siblings make for good memories, so thanks to Bob and Becky; Jean and Bill; and Cindy, Robbie, Debbie, and Mike, along with their spouses, children, and grandchildren. I'm getting to the point where there are too many to name—a sure sign that abundance is the true nature of grace.

Finally, for her invaluable help with this book (she has a keen editorial eye) and even more invaluable help with life and love (she has an overflowing and kind heart, which makes for the best home of all), I thank Terry, my wife. Every day she is with me is a good day.

Love Inspired®

HEARTWARMING INSPIRATIONAL ROMANCE

Contemporary,
inspirational romances
with Christian characters
facing the challenges
of life and love
in today's world.

**NOW AVAILABLE IN REGULAR
AND LARGER-PRINT FORMATS.**

Steeple
Hill®

For exciting stories that reflect traditional values,
visit:
www.SteepleHill.com

LIGEN07R

SUSPENSE

RIVETING INSPIRATIONAL ROMANCE

Watch for our new series of
edge-of-your-seat suspense novels.
These contemporary tales
of intrigue and romance
feature Christian characters
facing challenges to their faith...
and their lives!

**NOW AVAILABLE IN REGULAR
& LARGER-PRINT FORMATS**

Steeple
Hill®

Visit:
www.SteepleHill.com

LISUSDIR10

HISTORICAL

INSPIRATIONAL HISTORICAL ROMANCE

Engaging stories of romance,
adventure and faith,
these novels are set in
various historical periods
from biblical times
to World War II.

NOW AVAILABLE!

Steeple
Hill®

For exciting stories that reflect traditional values,
visit:
www.SteepleHill.com

LIHDIR08